PRAISE FOR *DECANTING A MURDER*

"Filled with amusing characters, snappy dialogue and delicious wine pairings, this mystery delivers a fast, sophisticated ride with just enough twists and turns to keep readers guessing until the final confrontation."

—*RT Book Reviews* (4 stars)

"Nettmann's lead character Katie Stillwell, aka 'The Palate', as an amateur sleuth is a perfect pairing in this intricately crafted sommelier mystery. At turns fascinating and suspenseful, I was thoroughly captivated by the story and enjoyed every turn of the page. Uncork me another!"

—Jenn McKinlay,
New York Times bestselling author

"The quiet hillsides and vineyards of California's famed Napa Valley have produced many famous vintages over the years, and first-time mystery author Nettmann knows this territory well … The first in a very promising series."

—Brendan DuBois, multiple award-winning
author and three-time Edgar nominee

OTHER BOOKS BY NADINE NETTMANN

Decanting a Murder

A SOMMELIER MYSTERY

UNCORKING
a
LIE

DEDICATION

To sharing a bottle of wine with treasured friends.

A
SOMMELIER
MYSTERY

UNCORKING
a
LIE

NADINE NETTMANN

MIDNIGHT INK
WOODBURY, MINNESOTA

FIRST EDITION
First Printing, 2017

Cover design by Kevin R. Brown
Cover Illustration by Pierre Droal/Deborah Wolfe Ltd.
Editing by Nicole Nugent

Midnight Ink, an imprint of Llewellyn Worldwide Ltd.

Library of Congress Cataloging-in-Publication Data
Names: Nettmann, Nadine, author.
Title: Uncorking a lie / by Nadine Nettmann.
Description: First edition. | Woodbury, Minnesota : Midnight Ink, [2017] |
  Series: A sommelier mystery ; 2
Identifiers: LCCN 2016047105 (print) | LCCN 2016057262 (ebook) | ISBN
  9780738750620 (softcover) | ISBN 9780738752006
Subjects: LCSH: Wine—Fiction. | Murder—Fiction. | GSAFD: Mystery fiction.
Classification: LCC PS3614.E526 U53 2017 (print) | LCC PS3614.E526 (ebook) |
  DDC 813/.6—dc23
LC record available at https://lccn.loc.gov/2016047105

Midnight Ink
Llewellyn Worldwide Ltd.
2143 Wooddale Drive
Woodbury, MN 55125-2989
www.midnightinkbooks.com
Printed in the United States of America

ACKNOWLEDGMENTS

My deepest gratitude to all my readers. You make my dreams come true.

A heartfelt thank you to my wonderful agent, Danielle Burby, for her unwavering support and guidance.

A huge thank you to my terrific editor, Terri Bischoff, and the entire team at Midnight Ink, especially Nicole Nugent and Katie Mickschl. Thank you to Kevin Brown and Pierre Droal for my beautiful cover.

My sincere appreciation to my critique group for their advice, support, and camaraderie: Jennifer Bosworth, Brad Gottfred, Gretchen McNeil, and James Matlack Raney.

A special thanks to the following friends who read various drafts of this manuscript and provided valuable feedback: Melanie Hooyenga, Sara Spock, Laura Konopka, Kelly Garrett, Kelsey Hertig, Irene Phakeovilay, and Solomon Mangolini.

Thank you to my parents for more things than I could ever list on a page, and thank you to my husband, Matthew, for your constant support, love, and encouragement.

CHAPTER PAIRING SUGGESTIONS

One: Crémant de Loire—Loire Valley, France
Two: Brachetto d'Acqui—Piedmont, Italy
Three: Burgundy—Côte d'Or, France
Four: Torrontés—Salta, Argentina
Five: Vinho Verde—Minho, Portugal
Six: Lambrusco—Emilia-Romagna, Italy
Seven: Primitivo—Puglia, Italy
Eight: Muscadet—Loire Valley, France
Nine: Spätburgunder—Ahr, Germany
Ten: Châteauneuf-du-Pape—Châteauneuf-du-Pape, France
Eleven: Mâconnais—Burgundy, France
Twelve: Prosecco—Veneto, Italy
Thirteen: Pinot Gris—Willamette Valley, Oregon
Fourteen: Nero d'Avola—Sicily, Italy
Fifteen: Blanc de Blancs Champagne—Reims, France
Sixteen: Cabernet Franc—Sierra Foothills, California
Seventeen: Malbec/Cabernet Sauvignon Blend—Mendoza, Argentina
Eighteen: Cariñena—Aragon, Spain
Nineteen: Gavi—Piedmont, Italy
Twenty: Touriga Nacional—Alto Douro, Portugal
Twenty-One: Valpolicella Superiore—Veneto, Italy
Twenty-Two: Pinot Blanc—Alsace, France
Twenty-Three: Cabernet Sauvignon Blend—Colchagua Valley, Chile
Twenty-Four: Côtes du Rhône—Rhône Valley, France
Twenty-Five: Brunello di Montalcino—Montalcino, Italy
Twenty-Six: Syrah—Yakima, Washington
Twenty-Seven: Beaujolais—Saint-Amour, France
Twenty-Eight: Riesling—Columbia Valley, Washington
Twenty-Nine: Pinotage—Stellenbosch, South Africa
Thirty: Monastrell—Jumilla, Spain
Thirty-One: Assyrtiko—Santorini, Greece
Thirty-Two: Sauvignon Blanc—Marlborough, New Zealand
Thirty-Three: Riesling—Clare Valley, Australia
Thirty-Four: White Port—Douro Valley, Portugal
Thirty-Five: Icewine—Ontario, Canada
Thirty-Six: Vin Santo—Tuscany, Italy

ONE

Pairing Suggestion:

Crémant de Loire—Loire Valley, France

*A sparkling wine made primarily from the Chenin Blanc grape,
ideal for beginnings.*

❧

When bottles of wine are sold for large amounts of money, they end up in the news. Sometimes it's because the bottle was rare and other times the final price was noteworthy or even extreme. Yet the seller is never really emphasized in the articles. It's always the buyer.

The buyer, who paid thousands and thousands of dollars for a bottle of wine, often with the notion to safely tuck it away in a cellar where it might not be moved again. I understood saving special bottles for long periods of time, but to know that a wine would never be released from the bottle, never get to live out its purpose of being enjoyed and savored, always gave me a tinge of sadness.

This time I knew the buyer well. Paul Rafferty was a longtime customer of Trentino and although he had an extensive collection of unique bottles kept safely in his wine cellar, he was also known for occasionally opening rare wines, sometimes at the restaurant where I had the honor of uncorking the bottle and releasing the story.

Long before Paul's assistant, Cooper Maxwell, made a special trip to the restaurant with the dinner invitation, I knew that Paul had recently purchased a 1975 Chateau Clair Bleu because I had seen the announcement in the newspaper. Most people, if not everyone, in the wine world had heard about it.

A frequenter of auctions and a known wine enthusiast, this mention in the *San Francisco Tribune* wasn't the first time Paul's name had been in the news regarding a bottle of wine. A few years ago at an auction in New York, he had paid $5,000 for a 1982 Chateau Lafite Rothschild and the previous spring at an auction in London, Paul acquired a bottle of 1919 Château d'Yquem for $4,500.

But his recent purchase at a Sonoma County auction garnered a large sum after a bidding war erupted and Paul kept going until he was the victor, turning over $19,000 for a 1975 Chateau Clair Bleu valued at half that price. Paul made it clear during the bidding that he wasn't going to stop until he had the bottle. And now he did.

When Cooper said it was "a special dinner at Paul's Sonoma house with a special bottle of wine," followed by a wink, I knew Paul was going to open the Chateau Clair Bleu. We had talked briefly about the winery, located in the Côte d'Or region of Burgundy, France, during Paul's visits to Trentino and while he once asked if we had a 1975, it wasn't brought up again. I was well versed on Chateau Clair Bleu, but the 1975 vintage was not its best known or even close to its best year.

Although I always loved to know about each bottle of wine, the history of the winery, the weather that affected the grapes that year, the trials and tribulations of the winemaker, this time I wanted to know Paul's story in regards to this wine. There was a reason he paid double what the bottle was worth, and I was eager to hear why.

The sun was nearly down in the January sky as I drove through Sonoma County, a wine region located north of San Francisco and west of Napa Valley. Home to over 400 wineries, the diverse topography of Sonoma County includes coastline, hills, and redwood forests.

The vineyards were bare this time of year, the rows ghost-like until the grape leaves sprouted again in the spring. Even though it was missing the organized greenness that thrilled my heart when I drove through wine regions the rest of the year, there was still the promise of future bottles of wine. Even during the winter, the magic was happening on the vines, we just couldn't see it.

While there are many regions of Sonoma County, each one creating a variety of wines, my journey tonight took me through the historic Sonoma Valley. With wineries that date back to the California Gold Rush, Sonoma Valley is located between the Sonoma Mountains and the Mayacamas Range where the cool air rushes in from the Pacific Ocean.

It was also the area where Paul Rafferty had his house. Or at least one of them. He also had a residence in San Francisco, which is why he dined at Trentino. I wasn't sure how often he was in Sonoma, but it was where he wanted to open the bottle. Although it meant a night of skipping work—I had been taking on as many sommelier and waiter shifts as I could in order to pay my bills, which had spiked recently due to my travels for the Certified Exam—I wasn't about to turn down the opening of Paul's 1975 Chateau Clair Bleu.

Two last turns and I arrived at the address Cooper had given me. There it was, a palatial house on top of a small hill. Paul had alluded to his wealth, but we never talked about it directly. His dinner discussions were kept to food, travel, and of course wine. He was fascinated by it and wanted to hear the details of every bottle I opened, even if he'd ordered that particular one numerous times before. Sometimes he dined alone, sometimes he dined with Cooper, and sometimes he brought a guest whom he would refer to as "his special lady friend," though the women varied.

I pushed the button on the silver box set into the slate wall at the gate.

"Rafferty Residence," said a voice too quickly for me to distinguish who it was.

"Hi, this is Katie Stillwell."

"Ah, a name I know so well," Cooper's voice came through the speaker. "Some might say you're the coolest sommelier around. Do you agree?"

I laughed. "If you say so."

"Because you're here, does this mean you've finally allowed me to whisk you off your feet and take you to faraway exotic lands?"

"If I say no, do I still get to come in?"

The gate buzzed and opened. I pulled inside and parked, my damaged Jeep out of place next to the Lexus and Mercedes in the driveway. The driver's side was dented and scraped from an accident in the fall. I would get it fixed eventually, but I needed the money first and since the car was functional, it would have to wait. The dents gave it character. Maybe damage gives all of us a little character. Like the grapes in Sauternes with Noble Rot, a fungus that drains the water out of the grapes. Instead of destroying them, it produces a very sweet and highly prized wine. Damage could be a good thing.

The doorbell's chimes echoed throughout the house, like a warning with an attempt to keep it melodious. I waited as the bells continued, knowing that I could never have a doorbell like that. Life always sounding like an alarm.

This was the first time in my four years at the restaurant that a guest had extended an outside invitation and even though I wasn't working this evening, my Certified Sommelier pin still adorned the lapel of my blazer. I decided long before I earned the pin, awarded by the Court of Master Sommeliers after passing the rigorous exam, that I would wear it to every wine-related occasion, inside and outside of work.

The door opened and there was Cooper, his brown hair neatly trimmed. He was only a few years older than me, somewhere in his mid-thirties, and he wore a beige suit and a large smile.

"There she is, the girl of my dreams." We were not strangers by any means, as I had met him a few times when he had accompanied Paul to the restaurant, but we didn't know each other that well and I still couldn't get a good read on him beyond the flattery.

"Cooper, I'm sure you tell that to everyone."

"I don't, actually. But do you want me to stop praising you?" He raised one eyebrow. "Because I will if you really want me to."

"No." I smiled. "Keep the praise coming. You're fun."

"Ah, that's what I want all the girls to tell me. That I'm fun." He grinned. His personality was always friendly, open, and slightly flirtatious. Perhaps he was a Viognier, a floral white wine that could be dry or sweet.

"But in all seriousness, Katie, I'm glad you've come tonight. This dinner will be so much better with you here." He hugged me and kissed me on the cheek.

That was new. I didn't think we had ever hugged before. In fact, I was sure of it. We had only interacted at Trentino. And the kiss, well, that was a definite first. I paused, not stepping inside the house. I was not in the market for a boyfriend. My focus was on my Advanced Exam, the next step with the Court of Master Sommeliers. I had tiptoed around it with my last romantic interest, a Napa sheriff detective named Dean, but I needed to be upfront now. I needed fewer complications all around.

"Cooper," I said as I touched my cheek where he had kissed, "I don't—"

"Just a greeting, Miss Stillwell." He winked. "In case you were going to allude to what I think you were going to."

Maybe he knew me better than I thought. "Are you greeting every guest tonight that way?"

"Only the ones I like." He smiled. "As a friend, of course. However, it's nice to see you outside of the restaurant. Why aren't we getting together more often? We should." He straightened his posture, standing just slightly taller than me. "Now I'm under strict instructions to tell you that you are not to work tonight in any capacity."

"But what about the wine? I'm happy to help, especially with the specific bottle Paul wants to open."

"Nope. I'm serving tonight." Cooper pulled a wine opener out of his pocket and held it up. It was expensive, double hinged with polished wood. I had seen them in the stores for around $150. "As soon as I can figure out how to work this thing."

I reached for the wine opener I kept in my purse at all times, but Cooper stopped me.

"I'm kidding. You're not the only one who opens wine bottles on a regular basis, Katie. I'd like to say I'm Paul's personal sommelier, but I know that if I asked him, he would say it was you. But you're a guest tonight, understand? A friend in Paul's house, just like the other guests. No different. So relax and enjoy yourself. Got it?"

"Got it," I replied. It would be nice to be served, but I needed to make a conscious effort to not help with the wine, especially around

Paul. A step outside of my comfort zone, for sure. I touched my Certified pin and thought about taking it off, but decided to leave it on for the time being.

Cooper guided me through the marble hallway as the sound of my boots echoed around us. The boots, which lifted me up an inch, were comfier than heels and mostly hidden under the pants of my fitted black suit. Even though I was an invited guest, I had worn a suit just in case I was given sommelier duties. I felt most comfortable in pants instead of skirts when working the restaurant floor, a force of habit that extended outside the restaurant.

"There are a few guests already here having aperitifs in the lounge. When everyone arrives, we'll start the dinner. By the way, I have a small gift I want to give you later."

"A gift? What?"

"Later." He smiled.

We entered the lounge, a rectangular room with white couches and floor-to-ceiling windows. A man and woman were sitting next to each other on the couch while a second man occupied a nearby chair. Their conversation stopped and they all focused on me.

"This is Katie Stillwell," said Cooper. "We have Henry Diven." He motioned to the man in the chair. "Leanor Langley and Simon Watkins." He nodded at the couple on the couch.

The three guests barely shifted, each watching me like a hawk studying its prey. I was clearly the outsider in this group and not just because I was the youngest by at least a decade. My anxiety level started to rise, beginning as it always did with a sudden tightening in my chest, restricting my breath.

I approached strangers at tables every night, all night long, at Trentino, but I belonged there and the guests were happy to see me. This was definitely not Trentino.

I turned to Cooper, eager to divert the attention away from me or at least get a break from the stares.

"What can I get you to drink?" he asked before I could say anything else.

It was time to warm up the room. I put on my game face, the stoic and unreadable mask I wore when encountering uncomfortable or awkward situations. It was a professional and polite demeanor that hid any and all feelings. "What is everyone else drinking?" I said to Cooper as much to the other guests in the room.

Henry shifted in his chair and took a drink from his highball glass while Leanor turned to Simon and started talking. Nice.

"I see we're having cocktails," I said to Cooper, ignoring the silent treatment the guests were handing me.

"Yes, two Manhattans and one glass of Champagne. I'm sure Paul will also have a glass when he joins us in a minute."

"I'd love Champagne," I replied for two reasons. The bottle would already be open as one guest, Leanor, was drinking it and Paul had mentioned a few times that he brought in bottles from lesser-known houses in the Champagne area of France. Drinking a glass at Paul's would be a treat for the senses.

"Champagne it is. Take a seat." He motioned to the chairs. "I'll be right back with your drink as long as you don't critique my serving methods." He winked.

"Cooper, I'm sure your methods are second to none."

"Second to one." He pointed to me.

I glanced at the three other members of the room. There was a dark contrast from the warmth that Cooper exuded. "Actually, Cooper, I'll come with you."

"No, don't worry. Make yourself comfortable and I'll be right back." He smiled and walked out of the room.

I was left to interact with guests who quite possibly didn't want to interact with me, but perhaps wine could change that. I'd found that talking about wine was a great icebreaker in nearly every situation.

Because Simon and Leanor were still entrenched in their conversation about a friend who had just launched a new business, I chose the chair near Henry, a thin gentleman in his early fifties with salt-and-pepper hair.

He watched as I sat down and then extended his hand. "I'm Henry."

"Katie Stillwell," I replied. My mother had always told me it was polite to say my full name during an introduction, though I still forgot now and then. I glanced at his glass. "I love Manhattans," I said in an effort to jump start a conversation. When wine wasn't an option as a topic, cocktails could be a close second. I knew the ingredients of all classic cocktails for my exams, so I was well versed on the subject.

Henry smiled as he swirled his Manhattan, the large piece of ice clinking against the glass in a mixture of whiskey, sweet vermouth, and Angostura bitters. "They're great, aren't they?"

"Do you prefer them made with rye whiskey or bourbon?" You could tell a lot about a person the way they ordered their drinks.

Henry stopped swirling as he thought about the question. I could tell from his expression that he wasn't used to this type of small talk. "I guess I prefer a classic Manhattan," he replied. "How do you know Paul?" Either he didn't want to talk about whiskey or he was unsure of me. I had a feeling it was the latter. "I haven't seen you at one of his dinners before," he continued. "It's rare for Paul to bring someone new into the fold."

I opened my mouth to reply, but Cooper stepped forward with the Champagne. "She's a friend of ours," he interrupted as he handed me the glass. "She enjoys wine, like everyone here, so Paul and I invited her to join us tonight."

The comment made me smile. I really was just a guest. Not an employee of a restaurant they frequented, instead I was introduced as a friend. The answer seemed to appease Henry and he continued to nurse his cocktail.

"Are you Cooper's new fling?" asked Leanor, who was ready to finally acknowledge my presence or at least find out more about me. She was in her early sixties, though her face had been doctored in an effort to retain her fading beauty, and her jet-black hair fell in a perfect horizontal line along her jaw.

"Only in my dreams," replied Cooper. "Now if you'll excuse me for a moment, I'll go wait at the front door for the remaining guests."

Leanor extended her hand, four large rings adorning her fingers, each with a different-colored jewel stone. "Leanor Langley," she stated and placed her hand in mine in a way that showed she was used to having it kissed. I shook her limp grasp. I didn't like super strong handshakes that hurt but I also wasn't a fan of weak ones.

She pointed to the bald man sitting next to her. "This is Simon." His absence of hair combined with his sharp features made it difficult to place his age, but I assumed he was in his fifties or sixties.

"Nice to meet you, Leanor and Simon." A trick my mom had taught me to remember names was to repeat them right after hearing them. She was a social butterfly compared to me and her hints came in handy. I used this one nightly at Trentino and it was helpful in making guests feel appreciated and welcome. "Leanor, that's a unique name. I don't think I've heard it before."

She waved her hand, her rigid posture not changing as she moved, and took a sip of her Champagne before answering. "My mother named me Eleanor. I hated it so I changed it."

"She does what she wants," added Simon, but he didn't smile when he said it. Lovely, a dinner with tension. This would be an interesting night.

"Paul hasn't mentioned you before. Do you live here in Sonoma?" asked Leanor.

"No, I'm in the city."

Leanor gave an almost imperceptible nod and if her eyebrows were capable of rising, they would have. "Is that how you know Paul?"

"Ah, yes," I replied. I wasn't sure how much information I should give. Cooper, and Paul, wanted me to be a guest.

"Simon," said Leanor in a bored tone, "you're going into the city soon, aren't you?"

Simon nodded as he raised his eyebrows. "Tomorrow."

"Bring me back more of those fudge truffles. Same ones as last time."

"As you wish," he replied.

Now that the focus was off of me, my shoulders relaxed and I settled into the chair. I looked at the golden liquid in my glass, the streams of minute bubbles ascending to the top. The Champagne was high quality, as I would have expected from Paul, and I reveled in the delicate taste as I sipped.

"I live in the city, too," said Henry. "Whereabouts are you?"

I lowered my glass. "I'm over near Golden Gate Park. You?"

"Marina District." Henry smiled but he seemed to study me as he did it. "Single?"

My stomach dropped. "Excuse me?"

"Just a question. I'm single. Not that I'm looking, but it's nice to meet someone whose relationship is not complicated like these two." He motioned to Leanor and Simon.

"Shut it, Henry," said Leanor.

Henry laughed while Simon remained unwavering in his expression.

I looked around for Cooper or Paul as I took another sip of my Champagne. Either of them would be a welcome change.

"So, Katie Stillwell," remarked Simon in a tone that emphasized both my first and last name. "What do you do? For work, I mean. You do work, correct? Or are you a lady of leisure like Leanor here?"

"What leisure?" replied Leanor. "My days are saturated."

"Saturated with what?" asked Simon. "Liquor?"

"You know as well as I do that I don't drink before noon." She turned to me. "Yes, what do you do?"

Game face on, I nodded. "I work as a—"

Paul Rafferty's entrance stopped me mid-sentence. He was the type of man who changed the atmosphere of a room the minute he entered. He exuded power but also generosity and he carried an air of energy with him wherever he went. A ruddy gentleman in his sixties, he loved telling jokes, always throwing his head back as his belly jumped with every roar of laughter. If I thought of him like a wine, I would say that Paul was a Tawny Port—aged and sweet and not appreciated by everyone. But he always took time for me. Needless to say, he was my favorite customer at Trentino and it didn't hurt that he also tipped very well.

"Now, now," said Paul. "Did Cooper not tell you the rules for tonight? We're not talking about work or jobs. You asked what Katie does? She's a guest. As are all of you. I want this to be a pleasant evening, away from work. No business talk." He glanced around, his

12

pale blue eyes surveying the room. "Speaking of guests, we're still missing three. Let's hope they arrive soon. There's a bottle of wine that's been waiting decades to be opened."

"Is that why we're here?" asked Leanor.

"You didn't know?" responded Simon.

She shrugged and downed the rest of her Champagne, placing the empty glass on the coffee table in front of her. "When Paul extends an invitation, I come. I didn't think there had to be a reason."

"Like Pavlov with a bell," added Simon.

"Shut it, Watkins. Or I won't take you to Paris with me."

A smirk formed on Simon's face but he tried to hide it by drinking more of his Manhattan.

Leanor turned to Paul. "Tell us about this bottle."

"We'll get there," replied Paul. "I want to wait until we're all here."

"Can't I know anything?"

Henry leaned forward in his chair. "Leanor, he won it at the auction last week."

"Do you win at an auction or do you buy? I've often thought *win* was a strange word," said Leanor.

Simon rolled his eyes, Henry swirled his glass, Paul smiled, and I remained silent.

"No takers? Fine. Which auction?" she asked.

"Do you not read the papers or does news only interest you if it's about who wore the latest fashion trend to the gala?" Simon said.

Leanor gave a sideways glance to Simon and then straight ahead at the wall, her lips rubbing together as if she was biting her words or perhaps using the remnants of Champagne as a lip gloss. I liked to think it was the latter but I knew her type well enough to know it was the former.

13

Cooper entered the room, bringing a sudden flow of warmth and energy. Three people, two men and one woman, were with him.

"The last of our guests," said Paul. "Welcome. Glad you could make it. The tortoise did beat the hare, so I guess it's not all bad being slow," he said, followed by a bout of laughter and then a wicked cough.

"You okay, Paul?" asked Henry.

"I'm fine. The only thing I'm struggling with is old age." He looked at me as he said it, most likely because I was the youngest one in the room. "Okay, since Katie is the only one who doesn't know everyone, let me do some introductions. First, this is Katie Stillwell. She's our special guest tonight."

I nodded at the three new people, all close to the same age as Paul.

"Katie, this is Roberto Morini." Paul motioned to the well-dressed man standing next to him, who stood about a foot shorter than Paul but with a grin twice as big.

"Alicia Trager."

Alicia smiled at me at the sound of her name. Her blond hair, which curled at her shoulders, reminded me of Mrs. Cleaver from *Leave It to Beaver.*

"And her husband, Martin."

Martin flashed a quick smile but he looked either unimpressed or bored to be there. Or perhaps it was his game face. The service industry wasn't the only one to have them. I wondered if he would drop it as the dinner progressed, but that made me wonder—would I drop mine?

"Everyone, take a seat and Cooper will get you drinks. I would recommend Champagne but I see a couple of our guests have chosen cocktails."

"Don't act like you don't love a good Manhattan as much as the rest of us," said Henry.

Paul grinned. "Guilty. After we've enjoyed our drinks, we'll move to the dining room for the real reason I brought you here tonight."

"The real reason?" asked Alicia. "You're not dying, are you Paul?"

"Not today, Alicia."

But as we sat in the lounge, those words resounded in my ear. As a sommelier, you know as soon as you approach a table what they're going to be like. From the way people look at you to how they are sitting to the questions they ask. As I looked around the room, something about this table felt very, very wrong.

TWO

PAIRING SUGGESTION: BRACHETTO D'ACQUI—PIEDMONT, ITALY

*A sparkling red wine made from the Brachetto grape
with hints of strawberries as things start to get darker.*

⌘

THE NEXT ROUND OF drinks was interrupted by the announcement that dinner was ready. We filtered into the dining room, where a sizeable glass chandelier hung over the center of the table.

"I thought you were going to get rid of that," said Alicia as she pointed to the chandelier.

"What can I say, the ex-wife's tastes are still around." Paul glanced up at the thousands of glittering crystals. "One day I'll remove it, but for now I'll keep it hanging over my head." He laughed at his statement.

I walked around the nine settings at the oblong table, one at the head for Paul and four on each side, checking the nametags written in calligraphy until I found my place, the last chair on the left side with Cooper next to me.

"Anna will bring out the food, so make yourself comfortable." Paul sat down and folded his hands together, looking quite pleased with himself. Simon was to his left, followed by Leanor, Cooper, and then me.

Alicia sat across from me, with Martin to her left, then Roberto, and Henry next to Paul.

"Here." Cooper handed me a large envelope as he sat down. "My gift."

"What is it?"

"If I told you, it wouldn't be a surprise, would it?"

I opened the envelope and took out a packet of different-colored index cards.

"You've mentioned at the restaurant that you're always studying flash cards at home. I know they're important to you and I saw these and thought of you."

I couldn't remember the last time I had been given a gift. I was definitely touched, but it also made me rethink Cooper's statement at the front door of just being friends. "That's very sweet." I put the cards into my purse. "Thank you."

"What are you studying for?" asked Henry.

"I think I've seen you somewhere before," interrupted Alicia as she cut off Henry's question.

"Oh?" I tried to remember if I had seen her at Trentino, but she didn't strike a chord of familiarity. "I have one of those faces. People always think they know me."

Alicia slowly nodded but continued to study me. "Do you live in Sonoma?"

"In the city," said Leanor with a hint of disapproval.

"Well, I love San Francisco," said Martin with the first indication of his fading game face. He looked genuinely happy to talk about the subject. "Are you from there?"

"No, but I've lived there for about four years now."

Alicia smiled. "What brings you out to Sonoma?" Her question puzzled me and I wasn't sure how to answer. Did she mean Sonoma in general or tonight for the dinner?

"Clearly," said Roberto, speaking for the first time, a thick Italian accent marking each of his words, "it's for the magnificent wine in this region. Correct, Katherine?"

I nodded. I wasn't used to being called by my full first name, but the way he said it made me smile. "Wine is the key to everything."

"I absolutely agree," said Martin.

Leanor shifted in her chair. "Considering your store is in Napa, Roberto, I'm surprised you wax so poetic about Sonoma."

He chuckled. "My heart is with both, Leanor."

A door from the side, which I assumed to be the kitchen, opened and Anna appeared holding two plates. She was close to college age and wore a white chef's coat and a chef's hat. She placed one plate in front of Leanor as the scent of beef wafted toward me. It wasn't long before I could see the expertly prepared meal as Anna put the second plate in front of me, heat emanating from the sides. Filet mignon, mashed potatoes, and a pile of sautéed green beans.

I heard Alicia scoff and I looked up.

"I don't eat meat," she said with her eyes still focused on my plate.

Paul laughed. "You think I don't remember?" He grinned as he leaned back in his chair.

Alicia smiled but it wasn't until Anna placed a bowl of penne pasta in front of her that her expression looked genuine.

I looked at the filet mignon in front of me and although I was certain it would be the highest-quality meat, I was secretly jealous of Alicia's penne covered with marinara sauce. I loved pasta. I was a self-described carboholic.

When every guest had a plate of food, Paul stood up. "Now, the pièce de résistance." He stepped to the side and gestured to the bottle of 1975 Chateau Clair Bleu on the sideboard behind him. "The moment you've all been waiting for. Or maybe you haven't, but I certainly have." He motioned to Cooper. "Will you do the honors?"

Cooper stood up as I tried to hide my disappointment. I would have loved to open the Chateau Clair Bleu. It thrilled me to open old wines and reveal a moment of history.

I leaned forward to suggest it to Paul but stopped myself. I was a guest tonight and I should get used to it.

Paul continued speaking as Cooper cut the foil off the top of the bottle. "When I first heard about Chateau Clair Bleu, there was no way I could afford it. I was barely scraping by." He glanced at each of us around the table. "Being able to purchase this wine, this particular one, means so much more to me than just a bottle of wine. It shows how far I've come. This wine has been waiting forty-two years, just like I have been working forty-two years. Finally, tonight, we meet."

Cooper picked up the wine opener and I felt myself twinge with jealousy. He positioned his opener over the top of the bottle, but the age of the cork, the forty-two years, jumped into my mind. "Cooper?"

"Katie?" Paul raised his eyebrows and I realized I had spoken louder than I intended.

"I'm sorry, Paul. I have a hint for Cooper."

Leanor whispered something to Simon but I ignored it.

"If I may." I stood up and approached the head of the table. "The cork is old and might crumble into the wine during opening if you use a standard opener. I don't want that to happen to your wine."

Color flooded Paul's face as he nodded. "I wouldn't want that to happen either. Thank you."

I examined the cork. It looked like it was in great condition but it still wasn't worth the risk. "Do you have an ah-so?" I felt the energy of the room shift followed by whispers.

Paul motioned with his hand to the drawer and I pulled it open. Inside was a variety of wine tools including an ah-so, a device that resembles a PI symbol. The prongs are positioned to slide down both sides of the cork and safely remove it in one piece.

I handed it to Cooper and stepped back.

A nervous knot formed in my stomach as I watched him. A slip of the hand could cause the cork to fall or crumble into the bottle. Cork would not be ideal floating in any wine, especially a $19,000 bottle, but older wines sometimes had problems with corks, possibly even mold. I didn't know how much experience Cooper had with an ah-so and I didn't want the wine to be ruined.

Cooper glanced at me with a tepid smile. "I haven't used one of these before."

My concerns were confirmed and that was all I needed. I stepped forward. "May I help?"

Cooper looked up with relief. He turned to Paul, who seemed deep in thought.

"Paul, if I may," I said. "It would be a great honor to open this bottle for you."

Paul's face changed from pensive to elated. "Of course, Katie. I'm sorry," he said. "I wanted you to be a guest, but I didn't realize that I might be robbing you of an experience. Please proceed."

"Thank you," whispered Cooper as he stepped to the side and returned to his seat.

A thrill went through me as I maneuvered the ah-so into the bottle. I was back in my comfort zone. I had only used the tool a handful of times, but the experience paid off. I removed the cork without issue and placed it on the silver tray to the left of Paul. This was it. The wine was ready to share its story.

The sideboard had a decanter and Paul, being quite the traditionalist, had set out a silver lighter and a candle which would illuminate the neck for sediment.

Although Bordeaux wines were routinely decanted to avoid the sediment in the glass, Burgundy wines traditionally weren't, due to their fragile nature and the lack of need for aeration. But Paul had the decanter out for a reason.

"Paul, would you like me to decant, or shall I pour from the bottle?"

Paul looked at the decanter and then up at me. "Please decant. I prefer the ceremony of it all. It adds another element to this occasion."

"Understood." I lit the candle and held the bottle over it as I started decanting the wine. After forty-two years, the red liquid was finally released from its captivity.

When all the wine was in the decanter, I picked it up and looked at Cooper. "Did you want to pour?"

He smiled. "I will if you want me to, but I have a feeling you might like to do the honors."

"As long as Paul doesn't mind."

Paul gestured to the glasses.

As protocol with the host, I poured a small portion of the wine into Paul's glass so that he could taste it.

"Continue on," said Paul. "We're equals here tonight, no need for me to have the first sip."

There were nine of us at the table so although a bottle of wine normally contains five glasses, I went light on pouring so that all of us would have a share. I did the math and it roughly came out to each of us drinking a little over $2,000 dollars.

"How much is each glass?" asked Martin. Apparently I wasn't alone in my thoughts.

"Two thousand dollars," I remarked.

"How do you know that?" Leanor stared at me.

I wanted to reply that it was simple math, but instead I pretended I didn't hear the question and took my seat. I didn't want the focus to be on me. This was the moment for the wine to shine.

Paul raised his glass for a toast. "To good friends, to good wine, to a good life. To change up an old Irish blessing, may the road rise up to meet you, may the wind be always at your back, and may you forever share a special bottle of wine with treasured friends." He took a breath as he glanced at each face around the table. "It's an honor to share this moment with you, my dear friends, some who have come to me through work and some through wine. Each of you played a part in this celebration tonight, and I thank you for it."

He shifted his focus back to the glass in his hand. "Back in 1977, my job was delivering sandwiches to law firms in the area. I remember seeing a group of lawyers having lunch in their conference room. They were wearing expensive suits and they were drinking wine in the middle of the day. The bottle on the table? A 1975 Chateau Clair Bleu. I decided right then that one day I would become a lawyer and one day I would drink a 1975 bottle of Chateau Clair Bleu. That would be the moment that I knew I had made it." He stared at the glass with such pride, as if it were his own son. "It took a long time, but that moment is finally here." He raised his glass higher. "Let's not delay it any further. Cheers."

The nine glasses clinked together and it was the first chance I had to take a good look at the wine. I had been too busy pouring it to really take note of it. The color was different from what I expected. Darker. Stronger. As everyone drank for the toast, a feeling registered deep in my gut that something wasn't right with the wine. I pushed the feeling aside and took a sip.

At that moment, I knew. Whatever this wine was, it wasn't a 1975 Chateau Clair Bleu.

THREE

PAIRING SUGGESTION: BURGUNDY—CÔTE D'OR, FRANCE

An elegant wine made only from Pinot Noir and greatly influenced by the region's soil, weather, and vineyard location.

❧

I GLANCED AROUND THE table. The other guests were enjoying the wine, continuing on with their conversations, and proceeding with dinner. But I couldn't.

I swirled the wine and took a deep sniff. The bouquet nearly jumped out of the glass. Which wasn't right. The fruitful scents of wine dim as it ages. If this was a 1975 wine, it wouldn't be this fruit forward.

I held up the glass and tilted it so the white tablecloth was behind, leaving a clear view of the wine. Red wine faded from the rim over the years, the sides becoming lighter in color, almost more translucent. A wine that was over forty years old would have fading in the rim and a Pinot Noir wine, such as this one, would have slight tinges of orange and brown to the red. Both the rim of this wine and the color were strong, like a recent vintage.

I took a sip. There was a characteristic that I loved about older wines, a unique flavor only brought on by the aging process. A marker of the years it had been waiting. This wine's flavor was not from age and in fact, was something I couldn't quite place at the moment. Almost like pepper.

I stared at the glass and swirled it around, hoping that my senses deceived me even though I knew they didn't. My blind tasting had previously been rocked by anxiety, but I was in full control at the moment. I wasn't wrong.

"What do you think of the wine, Katie?" asked Paul from the head of the table.

I didn't want to ruin his party and spoil his moment by announcing my suspicions. Not until I was certain, and maybe even not then. "It's an honor to have it in my glass."

"You're not drinking it."

I swirled again. "As with all wines, I'm admiring it."

"Of course," replied Paul, and he visibly relaxed. "I'm glad you could join us tonight. I knew you would enjoy this."

"Thank you." I smiled. "May I see the bottle?"

"Absolutely." He handed the bottle to Simon, who passed it to Leanor, then Cooper, and finally to me.

The label was reminiscent of a wine from the 1970s; even ones that had been protected over the years often had some yellowing. I held the bottle up to the light and examined the sediment in the bottom. It looked like the amount of sediment a 1975 Burgundy would throw, yet the wine in my glass told a different story.

"Are you okay, Katherine?" Roberto leaned across the table.

"Yes, why do you ask?"

"You're focused on the wine. Studying it. Is this what the reference meant earlier, that you love to study?"

"I just love old wines." I needed something to take everyone's eyes off of me. "Paul, is this the oldest bottle you've tasted?"

"Oh no, I once had the pleasure of being at a dinner with two bottles from 1911."

"I think I was there," added Martin.

"Yes, Martin. Remember that?"

While Paul continued with his story, I held up my glass and stared at it again, the light bouncing through the red liquid.

"Okay, spill it, Stillwell," whispered Cooper. "Even people who live and breath wine don't examine a glass like you're doing right now."

"What do you mean?" I put the glass on the table, not wanting to reveal my doubts.

"You keep staring at it and although we don't know each other very well, I can tell from your expression that you don't like it." A sideways grin spread on Cooper's face, highlighting a dimple. "Let me guess, you've tasted much better. On a trip to France or something like that." He nudged me with his elbow. "Don't spoil it for us, let us think this is fantastic."

"It's fantastic." I faked a smile.

"Great," he said in his continued whisper. "That's what we'll tell everyone else. But your real opinion is?"

"It's fantastic," I repeated.

"Nope, not cutting it. I want the sommelier opinion."

I hesitated. "Tell me your thoughts first."

Cooper picked up his glass and took a sip. "It's okay. I don't think it's worth what Paul paid for it," he said as he looked over at a heated conversation between Leanor and Simon about who had tasted the oldest wine.

"No, it's not." I didn't have the heart to tell Cooper, but I also didn't have the heart to keep my game face on and I felt it start to slip.

He leaned closer to me and I met his eyes. They were amber and kind. "Wait," he said. "There's something else, isn't there?" He dropped his voice more. "Is something wrong with the wine?" He glanced around the table where everyone else was fixated on their own conversations. "You don't have to tell me if you don't want, but you can trust me."

I took a deep breath as I wavered from the professional attitude I carried while withholding my opinions at Trentino. In particular, when a couple brought a wine into the restaurant, one that they had been saving or was special to them, and paid the corkage fee only to have me open the bottle and immediately know that the wine was flawed. They had no idea, so I kept back the information and the couple enjoyed their special bottle. Sometimes it's better not to know the truth, but right now I felt the urge to confide in someone, to see if I was correct.

"Is it just me," I whispered to Cooper as a conversation about the recent Christmas parade filled the air, "or does this wine not seem as old as it should be?"

"Old?" Cooper repeated louder than I would have liked. He picked up his glass and looked at it. "How can you tell?"

I waited for the group conversation to continue before I replied. "The rim of the wine should be light. It fades as the wine ages," I whispered. "And there's quite a nose on this wine. It should lessen over the years, but it hasn't."

"But what does that mean? Was the wine not kept well or something?"

I took a deep breath before replying. "No. It means this wine isn't from 1975."

Cooper's eyes grew wide and he glanced at Paul. "I should tell him." Heat burned into my cheeks. "You said I could trust you."

"You can. I won't tell him it was you who figured it out."

I shifted in my seat as I looked at Paul's face. He was beaming as he sipped his wine. Would he want to know that he had paid a lot of money for something that wasn't legitimate? Would he be embarrassed? It wasn't fair. "If I were you, I would keep quiet. It's only going to hurt him."

"But he needs to know the truth." Cooper shook his head. "He's been tricked. He should know. Don't worry, I won't involve you."

I put my hand on his arm as a sudden thought went through my mind. "Cooper. What if I'm wrong?" I had been studying wine for years now and I knew the signs, but the distrust in myself, the self-doubt, always managed to stake a claim.

"I believe you," said Cooper. "Besides, I have a way I can find out."

"What is it?"

"Don't worry." Cooper shook his head and leaned over to Leanor next to him. "Do you like the wine?"

"It's exquisite," she remarked.

I noticed the rest of the conversations had stopped and everyone watched Cooper and Leanor.

"Agreed," added Martin.

"Do you not like it, Cooper?" asked Alicia.

"I do. I was just wondering about Leanor's opinion."

"Do you know a lot about wine?" inserted Simon.

"Well, some." Cooper motioned to Paul. "Working for Paul, I keep learning more."

Simon nodded. "What do you think about this bottle?"

My chest began to tighten. If Cooper continued down this road, I would be brought along. It was not the right time to share my suspicion, not in front of Paul and not in front of his friends.

"It's distinct," he replied.

Relief swept through me.

"Do you know, I had a Valpolicella the other day and I would have described it the exact same way," said Martin.

"Ah, my home," said Roberto.

"I love Italy," said Leanor. "It's been too long since I've been."

"You were there last summer," said Simon.

"Exactly. It's been too long."

The conversation had shifted away from the wine, which was a relief, but I stared at the glass as I ate my dinner that had turned cold.

"Katie, you're still not drinking." Paul wasn't smiling.

I picked up the glass and smiled at him. "Savoring every drop."

"I love the way you really appreciate the wine," said Roberto.

"Speaking of wine," began Cooper. "Roberto, have you ever come across a counterfeit bottle at your shop?"

I stopped chewing midbite and stared at Cooper. I wanted to nudge him or do a sideways kick under the table, but it would be too obvious.

"A counterfeit? No, no. Not at all."

"But surely one or two must have come into the shop. I hear they can be quite common."

Roberto nervously laughed as he looked around the table. "I've never had one in my store."

"But maybe you didn't know. If you did come across one, how would you deal with it?"

Roberto's face turned a shade of red. "Cooper, if you're implying that I don't run an upstanding business, then we need to talk."

I debated stepping in, but this entire scene was out of my comfort zone.

"I don't think that's what Cooper is implying, is it?" said Paul.

"No, not at all. I was just curious," replied Cooper. "Out of everyone here, you see the most variety of wines."

Roberto took a deep breath. "No, I've never seen a forgery and I don't approve of them."

"I agree," added Martin. "Fake wine hurts us all." He looked at me. "You must work in wine." He motioned to the ah-so on the sideboard. "I'm sure you agree."

I nodded, knowing that a counterfeit bottle of wine was inches away from me. "I think we all hope that what we're buying is authentic, no matter if it's wine or paintings or a car."

"Excellent point," said Martin. He smiled, but I couldn't help but notice the stares that came from Alicia and Leanor.

———

After dinner, we moved into the living room, the same place where I had enjoyed a glass of Champagne earlier, but now there was even more tension in the air. Guests flowed in and out of the room but I decided to take a seat on the couch. The wine was still on my mind.

"You know," said Alicia as she sat down next to me. "If you're into wine, you should come to the Roundtable Charity Dinner in two weeks. There's a special wine tasting as part of the evening."

"That sounds lovely," I replied, unsure if it was an invitation to an already sponsored table or a suggestion. Charity dinners usually came with high price tags.

"Wonderful. I'll put you down. It's six hundred a spot, but you can just write a check."

And there was my answer. I couldn't afford it even if I wanted to. "I'll have to look at my work schedule first." I politely smiled.

"Alicia," said Paul who stood nearby, "not everyone can afford a six-hundred-dollar dinner." Although his comment was supposed to be polite, conversations about money always made me cringe.

Alicia stood up now that I was no longer an interest to her.

Cooper joined me on the couch a few minutes later. "Your comment earlier," he said in a hushed tone. "About the wine. There was a second bottle Paul bought at the auction that came from the same dealer. I'm going to go get it and I'll bring it up here to you."

"I'll come with you."

"No. I don't want him to know."

"I'm sure Paul won't mind."

Cooper stood up. "Don't worry. I'll be right back." He touched my chin in a way that was more than just a friend. Perhaps there was more to Cooper than I knew.

I hadn't dated in a long time because there wasn't room for someone in my life. Not with work and studying. But I knew there could be, if I made an effort. Instead I usually pushed people away. Like Dean. He was kind, made me laugh, and even saved my life. He also let me be myself and managed to overlook my past. Not that we had ever dated but there had been something between us until it ended. Because of me.

The group conversation continued as it had at dinner with Leanor recounting her summers in Italy and the rest of the guests listening or at least pretending to listen. The whole evening seemed to be a masquerade of appearances. Even by me.

FOUR

PAIRING SUGGESTION: TORRONTÉS—SALTA, ARGENTINA
An aromatic and perfumed white wine with a dry finish.

᪥

ANNA BROUGHT IN SLICES of coconut cake, several layers high, while Paul poured glasses of Château d'Yquem, the only Premier Cru wine in Sauternes and the most expensive.

"Sauternes. It's a very French evening," said Roberto.

"I love sweet wine," said Leanor. "It matches my disposition."

Simon rolled his eyes and I held back a laugh.

"Leanor, are you free on Tuesday?" said Alicia as she poked a fork at her cake.

"I believe so." She removed her phone from her large purse. "Yes." She smiled.

"Want to meet for lunch?"

"Always," replied Leanor as she entered the date in her calendar. "Where?"

"How about the Fremont Diner? I've been wanting to go back there for a while."

"Splendid." Leanor finished entering the information and put her phone in her purse.

"Where's Cooper? He's missing dessert," said Paul with a hint of disdain.

"He's always excited by the cake," said Alicia.

"Cake enthusiast," said Leanor. "Not like him to miss the baked goods."

"Maybe he's in the bathroom?" said Martin.

"Please," exhaled Leanor. "Everyone is allowed his or her privacy."

"We all have to go sometime," said Martin.

"Not Leanor." Simon smirked. "Isn't that right, darling?"

Paul glanced around. "Does anyone know where he is?" His face was mixed with worry and annoyance.

I knew it was time for me to say something. "I think he went to the wine cellar."

Paul motioned to the bottle of d'Yquem. "I have enough wine here."

The group shifted their focus from Paul to me, as if they were waiting for my next move.

"I'm not sure," I replied. "I think he wanted to get another bottle?"

"Can someone go get him? I don't need him wasting time in the wine cellar when we're enjoying a party up here. He should know better."

Alicia swirled her fork around her cake, Leanor sipped her wine, Simon sat back in his chair, Martin had a blank expression, and Henry continued eating.

Paul looked around the room and then walked toward the hallway. I didn't want him to leave his party and I also didn't care to be alone with the other guests.

"Wait." I jumped up from the couch. "I'll go. You stay with everyone." I glanced down the hall. "Where is the cellar?"

"It's the second door down to the left." Paul picked up the bottle of Sauternes. It was nearly empty. "In fact, Cooper was probably right. We're going through this faster than I expected. Can you get another bottle of d'Yquem while you're down there?"

"Absolutely." I felt the eyes of the group on me as I left the room.

The door Paul pointed out was cracked opened two inches, but no light shone from the inside. I pulled it open enough to peek my head in. It was pitch black. Surely Cooper wasn't in there. I looked around at the other doors in the hallway, but Paul had specifically directed me to this one. I looked inside again.

"Cooper?"

Stairs descended into the darkness with the faint scent of wine. This was definitely the cellar. Now to find the light.

I felt along the wall at the top of the stairs, but the switch was nowhere to be found.

"Cooper?" I repeated but was met with silence.

I debated going back to the lounge and asking Paul for help, in particular in finding the light switch, but I didn't want to bother him when he was with his guests. I stared down the stairs. There was no way that Cooper would be down here in the dark, but I had to make sure so I could go back to Paul and tell him. I pulled the door all the way open in an effort to illuminate the area with the hallway light.

"Cooper, are you down here?" I took one step at a time as my heart began to pound. Ever since I had been accidentally locked in a closet when I was little, the dark terrified me. "If you're down there and you're hurt, give me some kind of sign, okay?"

I waited for a response, but there was none. I didn't have my cell phone since I generally left it in the car to avoid being disturbed, but I did have a lighter in my pocket from the decanting. I hadn't meant to keep it, but it was a force of habit to keep the wine tools out of the way of guests. I would make sure I put it back in the dining room later.

I struck the lighter and the flame came to life, shadows dancing along the wall. My chest tightened and my breathing became shallow, but I also knew this was ridiculous. There was nothing to be afraid of, but it was the "what if" that always got me.

"I'm coming down the stairs," I called out. I took one step at a time, the light illuminating a few inches in front of me. The stairs creaked and I shuddered with each sound. I was on the last step when the lighter went out. My thumb ached from holding it for so long. I switched hands and lit it again, the shadows flickering on the concrete floor.

That's when I saw the shoe.

It stopped me at first, the sight of a brown leather loafer on the concrete. Then I stepped forward, the dim light outlining the ankle, the cream-colored pant leg, and finally the rest of Cooper's body. He was splayed near the bottom of the steps as if he had fallen.

I scrambled to him and put my hand on his back. His body was warm and he was still breathing.

"Cooper, can you hear me? You'll be okay. Don't worry, you'll be okay. Everything will be fine." I wasn't sure if I believed the words I was saying, but I knew you should give an injured person comfort. Words were important, especially at a time like this.

I looked up the stairs toward the lit hallway. "Help!" I screamed. "Help!" I repeated. "Paul! Anyone!"

There was the sound of pounding footsteps and a blast of light as the steps of the cellar became illuminated with the overhead light.

"Katie?" said Paul. "Why are you in here in the dark?"

"It's Cooper. He's hurt. Call 911."

FIVE

PAIRING SUGGESTION: VINHO VERDE—MINHO, PORTUGAL

A refreshing white wine with low alcohol,
meant to be consumed young.

☙

THE AMBULANCE TOOK COOPER away as two deputies entered the lounge where we all sat in silence. My lungs tightened and I had trouble breathing until I had a close look at them. Neither one of them was Dean. I had met John Dean, a Sheriff's detective who goes by Dean, during an investigation at Frontier Winery a few months ago and although there had been some flirtation, it had stopped there. He had phoned a few times since then, but I was focused on my Certified Sommelier Exam and failed to return his calls. Now that the test was over, I should call him back, but I worried too much time had passed. Part of me worried about other reasons. That I didn't want someone getting too close. That I didn't have room in my life for distractions on my journey to Master Sommelier.

"I'm Deputy Adams, this is Deputy Garcia. Was anyone else hurt?"

"Don't be silly," said Alicia. "He fell down the stairs. We were all in here."

"Who found him?"

"I did," I replied.

Deputy Adams approached me as I stood up from the couch.

"You can stay seated."

I hesitated, not wanting to be ordered to do something, but also not wanting to seem difficult. I returned to the couch.

"Tell me exactly what happened."

I repeated the story, that Paul had wanted someone to go check on Cooper in the cellar and I had found him at the bottom of the stairs.

"He obviously tripped," said Paul. "I've told him not to take those stairs so fast. And in the dark, too. I just don't know why he was down there. We were in here and I had enough wine out. There was no reason to go into the cellar."

"He wanted to look at a bottle," I added. I felt everyone in the room turn and stare at me.

"What bottle?"

"The other one that you bought at the auction."

"Why?" asked Simon.

"How do you know all this?" remarked Leanor.

I put my game face on. "I was sitting next to him at dinner."

"Why would he want to know about the other bottle?" asked Alicia.

This was not something I wanted to reveal to the group and I felt the tension in the room had shifted to me. "I have no idea," I replied calmly.

"Mr. Rafferty, can you show me the stairs where he fell?"

Paul stood up, almost unsteady on his feet, his face pale. "Of course," he said. "Follow me." The three of them left the room as the rest of us sat there in silence.

"What's this about another bottle?" asked Henry after a long minute. He looked at me but then glanced at everyone else around the room.

"Maybe he was an alcoholic," replied Leanor. "Couldn't get enough."

"I don't understand why he would go look," said Alicia.

I kept my mouth shut. Something inside told me to keep my cards to myself.

Deputy Garcia returned to the lounge and stood near the wall.

The continued silence unnerved me and I turned to him. "Do you know Detective Dean from Napa?"

He shook his head. "Can't say that I do. We work with Napa a lot, but Dean doesn't ring a bell."

I nodded as my heart fell a little. It would have been nice to know how he was doing.

"Sorry about your evening," said Deputy Adams as he came back into the room. "We'll be in touch."

"You're leaving?"

"We've completed our primary investigation. It appears that it's an unfortunate accident."

"Thank you for coming," Paul said as he walked the deputies out. When he returned to the lounge, he stared at the rest of us. "I don't know what I should do now. Would Cooper want us to keep the evening going? I'm sure he feels bad for tripping and falling."

"I'll have another drink," said Leanor. "We can toast to Cooper."

"Leanor," replied Simon, "Cooper has been seriously injured. I don't think we should keep drinking."

Paul looked at each of our faces, but I kept mine emotionless. I was the new person in this group, the one who didn't belong. I wasn't about to share my opinion.

"Simon's right," said Paul. "We should probably call it a night. I'll go to the hospital now to check on Cooper."

I stood up but the ringing of the house phone made us all stop. We stared at the phone on the side table but no one moved.

"Shouldn't someone get that?" I finally managed to spit out.

Henry picked it up as Paul watched, not moving.

"Paul, it's the hospital."

He ambled over to the phone. "Hello? Yes, this is Mr. Rafferty. Yes. Yes. Wait." His hand covered his face. "Wait. No. No." He stood holding the phone, saying nothing. "Okay," he finally replied in a voice that came out as a whisper. "Thank you. Okay." Paul's hand shook as he put down the phone and his knees began to buckle.

Henry took Paul's arm and led him to a chair. Paul sank down with his head in his hands.

"What is it?" asked Alicia. "What did they say?"

"Cooper. Cooper didn't make it. He's gone."

Leanor walked swiftly to Paul, leaned over and wrapped her arms around him. I stayed on the couch and watched as Henry, Simon, Martin, Roberto, and Alicia one by one stood up to hug Paul. I would have hugged him, too, but I didn't feel it was appropriate. I was the outsider here.

While the rest of the group comforted Paul, I returned to the wine cellar stairs. The top stair was a little loose, but not enough to make someone fall down a flight unless they were super drunk. Which Cooper was not. But I couldn't see any other reason for him to fall.

SIX

PAIRING SUGGESTION: LAMBRUSCO—EMILIA-ROMAGNA, ITALY

A sparkling red wine that ranges from sweet, Dulce, to dry, Secco.

☙

WHEN I RETURNED TO my apartment near Golden Gate Park in San Francisco, the first thing I saw was the vase of half dead flowers still sitting on the counter. My dad's new wife, Natasha, had sent them when I passed the Certified Exam as a way to reach out and mend the relationship. It was a sweet gesture and although she had signed his name, I knew there had been nothing from my father. After learning a few months ago that it should have been me who was jailed as a teenager instead of my friend Tessa, he had stopped speaking to me. A cop's daughter didn't get arrested, but more importantly, a cop's daughter didn't break the law in the first place.

We didn't have the best relationship to begin with, never quite seeing eye to eye since my mother passed away, but his silence about the exam definitely stung. Even though I knew in my heart that he was proud of me for becoming Certified, until I had confirmation with a call, an email, or even a text, I couldn't be sure. At least Natasha had reached out, which is why I couldn't bear to throw away the flowers even though they were past the wilted stage. They were a constant yet almost sour reminder. And maybe I needed that. A reminder that not everything is perfect. Everything needs work.

Though I would never tell them, I always compared people in my life to wine. My dad was a Barolo, a wine with gripping tannins, due to his strong and stoic disposition, and my best friend Tessa was a Merlot, thanks to her previously damaged reputation. But I was still figuring out Natasha. I had only met her a handful of times, three to be exact, and I didn't really know her. The first time was when I went to Los Angeles and my dad invited her over to dinner and shared that they were dating. The second time was when they visited San Francisco and my dad announced that they were engaged. And the third was at my cousin's wedding, months after their own wedding which had taken place in Santa Barbara. Apparently it had been a small occasion at the courthouse. One might think even a small wedding would be a family affair, but I *was* the family and I wasn't invited. My dad said it was easier for everyone involved if they just got married at the courthouse. So they did. An elopement, so to speak.

Our three interactions had given me enough of an impression that Natasha made my dad happy and was in no way trying to replace my mom.

I stared at the white lilies, or at least what was left of them. My dad mentioned Natasha had come from a tough life, yet I hadn't found out what exactly. But she was very sweet and she accepted me immediately.

Riesling. Natasha was a German Riesling. Grown in the steep slopes of the Mosel in slate soil. Sweetness born out of rocks. And definitely a strong contrast to Barolo. A contrast that I welcomed.

I moved the flowers a little closer to the edge, in front of the stack of bills, two in the dreaded red envelopes that signified final notices. If I didn't get a handle on my finances, I would be forced to move away from the city. I loved San Francisco, I loved my job, and I loved my blind tasting group. Moving was not going to happen. Not if I could help it.

My eyes drifted to the Certified Sommelier certificate on my bulletin board. It signified the victory after studying so hard for the test and not passing it the first time. Next to it was a yellow stickie note with Dean's number.

Dean. Even though I had never called him back, I had taken the time to write down his number from his messages. And even though I had kept it, there was something to be said that I never entered it in my phone. It remained on a piece of paper, easily lost or thrown away. Always keeping a distance from everything.

I took the brightly colored index cards out of my purse and placed them on top of my flash card binder in the bookcase. And then there was Cooper. A gentle and compassionate guy I had never really taken the time to get to know, now vanished from this world. My breathing became uneven and I knew anxiety was rearing its ugly head.

I needed something to calm me but the only thing that usually worked was to go to a vineyard and stare at the organized lines of the vines, ready to create the magic that becomes a bottle of wine to be uncorked, swirled, sniffed, sipped, and eventually savored. But I didn't have a vineyard nearby; I was in the middle of San Francisco.

I had an idea. I pulled out the binder and started flipping through the pages of flash cards until I reached my hand drawn maps of the wine regions. But the tightness in my chest remained.

I continued to the photos taken during my travels in France. There were the organized rows I needed. I stared at the pages and then closed my eyes, imagining I was back in the vineyards with the smell of the vines, the warm sun on my face, and the breeze in my hair.

My breathing calmed until my memory returned to the events of the evening. The Chateau Clair Bleu and Cooper. I told him there was something wrong with the wine, he went to investigate and ended up dead. Part of me didn't believe it was a coincidence.

SEVEN

PAIRING SUGGESTION: PRIMITIVO—PUGLIA, ITALY

Often referred to as the same grape as California's Zinfandel,
the subject is up for debate.

I ARRIVED EARLY AT Trentino the next morning. Although I worked at the restaurant, it was also where my blind tasting group met twice a week and tested each other on wines. The group consisted of Certified Sommeliers preparing for the Advanced Exam, the next step in the Master Sommelier progress and significantly harder than the Certified. Actually, I shouldn't say that we were all preparing for the Advanced; Jackson was already an Advanced Sommelier but still attended our group. He said it was a way to practice for his upcoming Master's exam, but I think he liked helping us and we appreciated his knowledge and experience.

Our group met as the restaurant opened for lunch, but the Monday crowd was always light, which made it easy for us to take over the private dining room. There was a second, though much larger, room if the restaurant ever needed us to move but in the two years we had been meeting, it hadn't been a problem.

Bill was waiting at the table as I entered. He was my manager at the restaurant, the one who organized the tasting group, and always the first to arrive.

"Morning!" he said cheerfully.

"Morning," I replied as I carried the bottle of wine I had brought, its identity hidden by a paper bag. Each member of the group would take a turn to audibly identify one of the blind wines, followed by each of us agreeing or debating the call.

I poured the wine into the second glass at each of the five places, the first glass already filled with Bill's wine.

The door opened behind me and Jackson walked in, followed by Darius.

Although I compared everyone in my life to a wine, I didn't for my tasting group. Since we met twice a week to identify wines, it would have muddied the waters too much to relate them to varietals as well. So they were all just friends. Except for Kurt, who had yet to arrive. He was a California Zinfandel, but that was because we briefly dated before I joined the tasting group. A red wine with a raspberry jammy quality and a hint of pepper. Sweet but had some spice. Then again, didn't we all.

"Someone's late," said Bill with a smile. "We'll give him five minutes before we start."

Darius and Jackson started pouring.

"I vote we switch his glasses around." Darius pointed to Kurt's setting. "Serves him right for slacking."

The door swung open and Kurt walked in. "Sorry I'm late."

"I was beginning to think you'd left us," said Jackson.

"Or died," added Darius.

"Please no more deaths," I muttered.

The group stared at me.

"Did someone die?" asked Bill.

"Yes," I replied as a shiver went through me. "Last night. At the dinner I went to at Paul Rafferty's house."

"Who died?"

"Cooper. Paul's assistant. He fell down the stairs. It was terrible. Though, now ..." I paused, uncertain if I should reveal my suspicions about it not being an accident.

"He was a nice guy. I've met him a few times when he joined Paul," said Bill.

"I'm sorry to hear about Cooper, but does death follow you everywhere?" quipped Kurt as he poured his glasses. "Should we be worried?"

I looked at Kurt. He wasn't smiling. "No."

"This is the second one in a few months. Could've fooled me." He stared at me when he said it, the tone of his voice flat and even. This was out of character for him. I knew him well enough to sense that something was very wrong.

"You okay, Kurt?" asked Bill. So I wasn't the only one who thought that he was acting differently.

"Perfect." Kurt smiled but his grin was a knowing one. It was the same one he wore when he approached tables nightly as a waiter at Greco's, an Italian restaurant a few miles from Trentino. It was also the same expression he wore when I broke it off with him, as he tried to hide the pain I had caused. While his game face could fool others, it was like an open book to me.

"Spill it, Kurt." I waited for him to reply.

He shook his head as his smile faded. "They've cut my hours at Greco's. Looks like I need to start looking for an additional gig." His eyes flicked to Bill as dread washed through me. Although I adored Kurt as a friend, our romantic history would not be an ideal situation at work.

"You got anything here, Bill?"

Bill winked. "We might be able to find you some shifts. I can't promise it'll be a lot, but it'll be something."

"Thanks, I really appreciate it."

"Shall we get started?" I interjected. "There are five glasses of wine here that are begging to be identified."

"Chomping at the bit, are we?" said Bill.

I smiled without emotion. "Just keeping us focused."

"I agree, let's start," replied Jackson as he picked up a glass. "I'll go."

Jackson went through the grid, identifying the wine first by its color and structure, then by its scent, and finally its taste. We would have to do this for six wines at the Advanced Exam and all under a time limit. The most important part, at least for me, was to keep calm under the pressure.

I focused on the wine as I mentally explored the three possible varietals. Sancerre, Grüner Veltliner, and a dry Riesling.

"Final conclusion," said Jackson. "This is a 2015 Sancerre from Sancerre, France."

"Anyone want to disagree?"

"I do," I replied.

The whole group turned to me.

"What do you call it?" asked Bill.

"A Grüner Veltliner from Kremstal," I replied, noting a wine from Austria that was similar to the Sauvignon Blanc–based Sancerre. "I felt like there was white pepper. It's Grüner Veltliner."

Darius picked up his glass. It was the first indication that I was wrong. Darius had brought this wine and knew what it was. If I had been right, he would have just sat there. But picking up the glass and smelling it meant he was looking for the white pepper that wasn't necessarily there.

"Anyone else?" asked Bill.

"I'm going to go with Sancerre," said Kurt.

"Same," said Bill.

"Never mind." I sniffed the wine again, noting the lime. "I'm going to go with Sancerre, too."

"Okay, the reveal."

Darius held up the bottle covered with a paper bag, which he pulled off to reveal a Grüner Veltliner from Kremstal, Austria.

"Gotta trust yourself. You were right the first time."

I gritted my teeth, annoyed that I had changed my call.

"You're the Palate," said Darius, a nickname the group gave me a year ago due to my blind tasting skills. "It's not like you to falter like that."

"I know. I'm just rattled."

"About Cooper?"

"Yes." *And Kurt,* I wanted to interject, but I left it. This wasn't a scenario where I needed all of my points on the table.

"When you're in that test, there are going to be a hundred different things that will rattle you. You can't let them get to you," said Jackson.

"I know," I replied as I picked up the glass and took a sip of the Grüner Veltliner. There was the white pepper, lime, grapefruit, and strong acidity. I should have been confident in my call.

"You still have several months. You'll be able to master your nerves," continued Jackson. "You guys are signed up for the next exam, right?" He motioned to me, Kurt, and Darius.

We all nodded.

"You're continuing to study theory, right? It's a lot different from the Certified. The bar is set pretty high. Whatever theory you had before, dive deeper into it now. You know the main rivers, now learn the tributaries. You've studied the regions, make sure you know the classic producers in each one."

Kurt held up his phone. "I'm doing my flash cards all the time." He swiped to the next screen to display another electronic flash card.

Darius. "Me, too."

Jackson looked at me.

I decided to reply honestly. "Kind of. I'm compiling more and more flash cards, I think I have two thousand now, but I'm not fully studying yet."

"Katie."

"I know, I know. I looked at them briefly last night, but I'm going to focus on studying soon. Like this weekend. In fact, I'll take my binder with me to the park. I like it there, the facts seem to stick."

"Binder?" asked Kurt.

"Yeah, that's where I keep my flash cards."

"That's archaic. Why don't you switch to electronic ones like the rest of us?"

I looked at Kurt. "What's wrong with the paper ones? Not everyone uses the flash card programs.

"You're making more work for yourself."

"Don't critique my learning methods. We each have our own ways."

"Okay," said Bill. "Let's keep this tasting going. Katie, you want to go next?"

"Sure." I picked up the next glass and took a deep breath in an effort to focus myself before I began. Calm, cool, and collected. They were not descriptors that portrayed the real me behind my game face, but I was going to have to become them. But most importantly, I needed to trust myself.

EIGHT

PAIRING SUGGESTION: MUSCADET—LOIRE VALLEY, FRANCE

*A dry white wine made from Melon de Bourgogne grapes
and left sur lie (on the lees), which creates a rich and creamy feel.*

❧

WHEN THE TASTING GROUP ended, I opened the door of the private
dining room. Lunch was not a busy time at Trentino, with most
people selecting dinner as their meal of choice at the restaurant, but
I noticed Paul Rafferty in a corner booth.

"Paul's here today?" I whispered to Bill as we stood near the door.
"Does he usually come for lunch?"

"No. Not that I can recall. He doesn't look well. His health has
been declining the last year or so, and maybe with Cooper's
death … I don't know."

Paul's shoulders were down and he stared at the table as he
twirled a fork on the tablecloth. Not surprising for him to look
crestfallen since his assistant had just died. I would offer my condo-
lences again. That's the least I could do.

I approached the table. The vigor that Paul always exuded was gone, replaced not by a lack of energy, but a dark one. He sat staring, barely blinking. There was an uneaten steak on his plate. I don't think he had even taken a single bite of it, but I could tell from the way the juices had congealed on the plate that it had been there a while.

"Paul," I managed to stumble out. He looked up, his eyes missing the usual spark of excitement. I had approached his table many times over the years, but I had never seen him like this. "I mean, Mr. Rafferty."

"Katie." He stared blankly at me. "Don't," he said.

"Oh, sorry." I took a step back.

"No, I mean don't call me that. To you, I am Paul. There's no need for pretense. Especially now." His attention fell to the unopened wine menu on the table. "I'm sorry, it's too early for me to drink, but thank you."

"I'm not even . . ." I was about to say *working*, but it didn't matter. I would get him a drink if he needed one. "Paul, I know I said it last night, but I want to say it again. I'm so sorry about Cooper."

Paul's gaze left the table and he stared across the restaurant, looking nowhere in particular. "Cooper worked for me the past ten years. I don't know what to do without him. I thought coming here would make me feel better." He motioned around the restaurant. "But even Trentino seems dreary today."

"Mondays are pretty light overall, but if you come back for dinner, it'll be much busier."

Paul shook his head back and forth. "I just don't understand it."

"I know, it's not fair."

"No, I mean I don't know why he went down into the cellar to look at the other bottle. I didn't tell him to get more wine. I don't understand."

I took a sharp breath and glanced around the restaurant. All the tables around us were unoccupied. "Paul, there's something I need to tell you. I didn't want to share it last night in front of everyone, and to be honest, I wasn't sure if I ever would."

"What? What wouldn't you tell me?"

It felt strange, standing there at the table at Trentino but instead of delivering wine, I was about to deliver unwelcome news. It was as though I was betraying my job, and I didn't like it. I glanced over my shoulder one more time and then motioned to the seat across from him. "May I?"

"Please."

I sank into the booth.

Paul's forehead creased with deep lines as he waited for me to speak. "What is it?"

"I know why Cooper went into the cellar to look at the other bottle."

Paul shook his head. "Why?"

"Because of what I told him earlier that evening." This was it. I was about to ruin his dreams and ruin his special dinner, though with Cooper's death, it was already in shambles. I could keep the information about the wine being counterfeit to myself, but I wanted to tell him. I needed to tell him. Because I had started to wonder if Cooper's death wasn't just an accident.

"Mr. Rafferty. I mean, Paul. The bottle we opened at dinner last night. The 1975 Chateau Clair Bleu."

"Yes?"

"Cooper went into the cellar because I told him the wine was counterfeit."

Paul's face changed from grief into confusion. "Why would you tell him that?"

"Because—" I took a deep breath. "Because it's true."

Paul blinked slowly as the words sunk in.

"I knew the moment I picked up the glass. The wine was too new to be from 1975 and to be honest, I don't think it was from Burgundy at all." I explained how the indicators didn't match an older wine.

Paul stared at me, not moving. "This whole thing keeps getting worse." He shook his head and breathed out. "Why didn't you tell me last night?"

"With Cooper's death—"

"No," he interrupted. "Before then. When you poured the bottle. At dinner. Why didn't you tell me then?"

My gaze fell to the table. "That bottle meant so much to you. You were so happy to finally open a 1975 Chateau Clair Bleu. I didn't want to take that experience away. To rob you of that joy."

"Instead I'd already been robbed, or at least my wallet had been." He stared at the uneaten steak in front of him. "Nineteen thousand dollars for a bottle of nothing. To add further insult to injury, Cooper is dead."

"I'm so sorry. Both about Cooper and about the wine. I'd like to say you could contact the seller and get your money back, but with the wine gone, unfortunately so is the evidence. I don't think you could pursue anything."

Paul nodded.

"I should let you eat." I stood up from the booth.

Paul looked up at me. "No, I don't like that idea."

"What?"

"That I can't pursue anything." He shook his head. "Would you be able to tell if another bottle was counterfeit?"

"Maybe. As long as the indicators are there. Or should I say, not there. I mean, yes. Possibly."

"Good. Sit down."

I glanced around the restaurant and then slid back into the booth.

Paul pushed his plate to the side and leaned forward. "I don't like that I was tricked. Not just out of my money, but also my pride. I was cheated." He motioned to me. "You know wine. You knew that bottle was counterfeit and you can help me get to the bottom of this. What do you think? I'll make it worth your time."

"I wouldn't know where to start."

"How about my cellar?"

"Mr. Rafferty … Paul. I can take a look at the bottles you have, but unless they were opened, I don't know if I could tell if they are counterfeit. The people who do this are very good at duplicating labels or even refilling older bottles, which is what I think might have happened with the Chateau Clair Bleu." I put up my hand. "And before you say anything, I'm not going to open up the bottles in your cellar. I would assume that most, if not all, of them are legit."

Paul nodded.

I took a breath. "Even the one Cooper wanted to take a look at. The second bottle from the auction. I wouldn't want to open it in case it was real. I don't want to take that risk."

"I understand," said Paul. "But what if you look into the bottle that I already bought and opened. The 1975 Chateau Clair Bleu. Find out who is to blame."

"And then what? I can't stand there and accuse them. That won't go over well. And I …" My voice fell away. I couldn't tell him that I had my wine reputation to worry about. I didn't know how that would sound.

"No, you wouldn't have to accuse them at all. Find out who's behind it and then I'll go after them with legal action." Paul's expression was full of hope and no matter what I thought about the offer, I was already involved in some way.

I took a breath. But I had no idea how to get to the bottom of wine fraud and I needed to spend all of my free time picking up extra shifts. I had to make sure I was able to pay my bills. "Although I would love to, I have my job here and I'm studying to take the Advanced Sommelier Exam later this year. I don't know how much time I would have to look into the wine."

"I'll pay you a month of Cooper's salary," Paul interjected. "It'll take me at least that long to find a new assistant."

I didn't know how much Cooper earned, but I was certain it would be enough to help with a bill or two. And if it only took me a few days to figure it out, it wouldn't affect my work or studying. "Okay," I said. "I'll do it. I need to manage it around the time I'm here at Trentino, but I'll help you."

"Thank you, Katie. You don't know how much this means to me." Paul cut into his steak. "I didn't think I would get my appetite back, but suddenly I'm hungry. Thanks to you. Because you're going to help me." He took a big bite, a smile on his face as he chewed.

"I'm glad." But as I thought about it, I had no idea where to begin. Maybe I needed to tackle it like an unknown wine, a rare varietal sure to trip me up during the Advanced Exam. Stop fearing the unknown and pick up the glass to look for the clues. Or in this case, the bottle. "Paul, where is the empty bottle from last night?"

"It's still at the house in Sonoma."

"Okay." Along with the second bottle from the auction. It would take me at least an hour to drive there and Paul was here, so I needed another place to begin. "You bought it at the Sonoma County Red Heart Charity auction, correct?"

"Correct." Paul took another bite of his steak and my stomach turned. Cold steak was not exactly appetizing.

"Who was the seller at the auction?"

Paul shook his head. "I don't know. It was a private party. When they don't want to be known, they aren't."

"You're giving me a dead end here."

A small smile slowly appeared on Paul's face. "Not exactly. You should go talk to Henry Diven."

"Henry?"

"He was in charge of the auction. You didn't know?"

I shook my head. "You wouldn't let us talk about work at the dinner."

"That's right. It was supposed to be a fun evening…"

I wanted to distract him before he became sad again. "Where is his office located?"

"He works out of his home. Not too far from here, actually."

"I'll start there. Can you call him and let him know I want to see him? I'll leave now."

Paul stopped eating. "Do you think that's a good idea? To go on your own, I mean?"

"Why?" I stared at him. "Is there something about him I should know?"

"No, he's been a good friend for many years. I just want to make sure you're okay doing this. I don't want to put you in any dangerous situations."

"Paul, if there is something about Henry I should know…"

"No, he's fine."

"So you'll call him?"

"Yes." Paul pulled out his phone.

"Wait." I put my hand out. "What are you going to tell him?"

"What do you mean?"

I thought about it for a moment. "Don't tell him I'm investigating. If he was in charge of the auction, he knows the seller and if he says something to them, they'll be able to cover up their tracks before we get to them."

"You're very clever, Katie. I'm glad you're working for me." Paul beamed in the same way my dad used to. It made me feel like my dad was proud of me. Which he wasn't, at least as far as I knew.

"In fact, I don't think you should tell anyone about the wine," I added.

"I agree." Paul held his phone, ready to call. "Any thoughts on what I should tell Henry then?"

I tapped my fingers on the table as my eyes drifted to the glass wine cellar in the restaurant. "Does Henry have a wine collection?"

"Yes, an extensive one."

"Perfect. Call him and say that I'm working for you. That I'm going to expand your wine cellar. You've hired me to help with it and I want to check out his collection, or something like that."

"Ah, great idea. I know what to say. He has a bottle of 1958 Chateau Mouton Rothschild that I've wanted for a long time. He keeps hinting about selling it, but then says he's not ready to part with it. I'll tell him you want to look at it."

"Couldn't you just buy a 1958 at an auction?"

Paul smiled and leaned in closer. "This one is special. It's signed by the artist who did the label that year. Salvador Dali."

NINE

PAIRING SUGGESTION: SPÄTBURGUNDER—AHR, GERMANY

A Pinot Noir wine with essences of cherry and earthiness.

ROAD CONSTRUCTION SLOWED MY journey, but twenty minutes later I arrived at Henry's house, located not far from the Marina District in San Francisco.

It had a quaint exterior dotted with meticulous flower boxes, which continued down the steps. Someone, probably Henry, spent a lot of time caring for the garden and I immediately guessed that the inside of the house would show the same amount of attention.

As I exited my car, Henry stood in the front doorway, watching me. A warning registered in my gut. I was supposed to trust my instinct, but I decided to push it aside in order to help Paul. I walked up the steps.

"Welcome," said Henry with a strange half-smile on his face. "I'll admit, I was rather excited when Paul called and said you wanted to see me. I didn't think we hit it off at the dinner, even before Cooper's tragedy."

"Yes," I replied. "There was so much going on that night, I think impressions were muddled. But I'm glad I'm here, Mr. Diven."

"Henry, please." He motioned to the door behind him. "Come inside. Can I give you some tea or perhaps a glass of wine? It's after twelve so it's acceptable to start drinking. However, I don't think the time stops many of us in the wine industry, now does it?"

I smiled and stepped inside the house. The inside was surprisingly modern, a different turn from the picturesque look outside. As if Henry liked to put out an image that people wanted to see, but actually enjoyed a different side. The contrast was not lost on me.

"So what can I get you? Red or white?"

I glanced at Henry. "Thank you, but it's not necessary."

"Are you sure?" He pointed to the glasses lined up on the bar.

"I am."

"Shame," Henry replied as he motioned to the bright red couch in the living room. "Would you like to take a seat?"

I sat down, but I kept on the edge of the cushion as I didn't want to appear too comfy. "I wanted to talk to you about—"

"Are you sure there's nothing I can bring you?" Henry interjected.

"No, thank you."

"Okay then." Henry sat down on the triangle-shaped chair across from me. "Paul said you wanted to talk about a bottle of wine? I think now that he's had the 1975 Chateau Clair Bleu, he's hungry for his next quest."

"Yes," I said as I realized I had been presented with an opportunity. "Since you mentioned the Chateau Clair Bleu, now that Paul isn't here, what did you think?"

Henry shrugged. "I thought it was fine, but not quite my taste. I would have preferred something a little more tannic to go with the filet mignon. Of course the thing that really comes to mind is poor Cooper falling down the stairs."

"Yes," I replied. "It's heartbreaking."

Henry waited for a moment and then clapped his hands together. "So, what wine are you here for?"

"Wine?" I wanted to find out more about the 1975 Chateau Clair Bleu and not the Mouton Rothschild Paul had referred to, but I needed to stick to my story. Except I couldn't remember what year Paul had mentioned. This wasn't like me. But it wasn't time to panic. Even if I couldn't remember, there were other ways to get to the answer. Like in the service portion of my next exam, even if I didn't have the answer, I needed to think on my feet. And I could do this.

I took a breath and put on my game face. "Paul was interested in adding another bottle to his collection. One that you have in your possession. A Chateau Mouton Rothschild."

"Ah, the 1958. He's been wanting that bottle for years."

"Yes, that was it," I said with relief. "The 1958 Chateau Mouton Rothschild."

"I'm sorry to inform you that it's not for sale. It means too much to me." Henry tilted his head. "Why did he want you to look at it?"

My thoughts raced. "I'm working on a project for him, helping him expand his wine collection."

"Makes sense since Cooper's gone. But as I said, the bottle isn't for sale. Paul knows this."

I nodded. "I think he was hoping you would change your mind."

"Nope." A thin-lipped smile formed on Henry's face. "Are you here to change my mind?"

A chill crept up my neck. "No."

"It might be open to changing…" Henry relaxed into his chair. "I'm glad you're here." He smiled knowingly and I didn't like it. "Well?"

"Well, what?" A warning bell was ringing inside me.

He sat up in his chair and leaned forward. "Shall we get to business and go downstairs?" he said, his voice almost a whisper.

"Excuse me?" Heat rushed up my neck.

"You know what I'm talking about." He winked. "It's what you came here for."

My reason for being there dissolved as I was suddenly very aware that I was alone in a house with a man who seemed to think I was there under romantic pretenses. Paul had hesitated when I said I was coming here alone. I didn't know Henry and I needed to keep my wits about me.

I stood up. "I think I should go."

"Wait, why are you leaving? What about the bottle?"

"I wish we were still talking about the bottle."

"I'm sorry?" Henry shook his head. "I don't understand. You came here to ask about the Mouton Rothschild. Don't you want to see why Paul wants it? It's a special bottle. What's the problem?" He looked genuinely confused and I was genuinely mistaken.

I sat down and put my face in my hands, my cheeks burning. I had read the situation completely wrong. I faked a cough to explain the lapse of poise and recomposed myself. "Yes, I would love to see the bottle."

"Great. We'll go downstairs. I'd love to show all of it to you."

I hesitated as I thought about how my best friend Tessa would reply to that comment. Tessa was a serial dater and would have encouraged the situation with a snarky reply. I held back a laugh. "Your wine collection?"

"Yes. I have prized bottles from all over the world. I keep them downstairs to avoid the light and temperature changes that could affect them. Has Paul told you why the Mouton Rothschild is so special?"

"It's signed by Salvador Dali."

Henry studied me. "Why would that be significant, do you think?" He was testing me. He didn't know I had nearly two thousand flash cards in my apartment with facts just like this.

"Because he designed the label. The Chateau chooses a different artist every year."

"You do know your wine, Katie Stillwell. You must work in the wine industry. Or perhaps you simply enjoy studying the wine collections of people like me and Paul?"

I stiffened. I was no longer a guest at Paul's dinner; people could know what I did now. I also felt the need to assert myself that I wasn't just a wine fan, but that I was a wine professional. "I'm a sommelier at Trentino."

"No kidding." Henry looked genuinely surprised. "That must have been the pin you were wearing last night." He stood up. "Come on, I'll show you the Mouton Rothschild." He headed toward a staircase at the far end of the house.

"Since you know wine," he said with an air of newfound respect, "you'll love the bottles I have down there. Not to brag, but many wine enthusiasts are jealous of my cellar." His statement didn't come across as cocky or arrogant, but passionate. He clearly loved his wine.

The cellar was located at the bottom of the stairs on the lower level of his house. Its position next to the hallway was where a closet might be. In fact, the door looked just like a closet.

"I know it doesn't look like much, compared to Paul's," said Henry. "But you'll see once you look inside." He pulled open the door to reveal an intricate racking system from floor to ceiling. Though the space was small and was definitely once a closet, there were at least two hundred bottles of wine from Bordeaux, Burgundy, Southern

Rhone, Germany, Spain, Italy, and more. It was a treasure-trove of wine packed into a cozy space.

"I disagree," I said as I glanced at the names. "Paul would be very jealous."

"He might be. I'm sure he has some bottles that would make me envious, too."

I nodded as the counterfeit wine went through my mind. I looked up and down the racks, admiring each bottle.

Then I saw them. Five bottles of Chateau Margaux.

They were halfway down one section of the racks, the markings '55, '62, '63, '68, '69 on the wood below them. A bottle of 1969 Chateau Margaux. It was the same wine I had enjoyed with my mother shortly before she passed away. I longed to relive the memory and once again taste the wine and pretend my mother was still alive, sitting next to me in the kitchen like all those years ago. The bottle continued to elude me primarily due to the price tag, yet here it was, staring me in the face.

"You okay?" asked Henry. "You're very quiet."

"No, I'm fine." I motioned to the bottles. "You have an impressive collection."

"You seemed to pause in the Bordeaux section."

I returned my focus to the Chateau Margaux. "Yes. The Margaux. It's nice that you have a few different vintages here."

"I pick them up at auctions when I can. Are you a fan?"

I nodded. "In particular," I pointed to the '69, "that one."

Henry reached for the bottle and pulled it out of the slot. "Not their best vintage, but a great one nonetheless."

There it was, the bottle I had wanted for years. Just inches from me. I took it from him, the cold glass contrasting with the warmth from my hands, the memory of my mother waiting inside. I wanted to take it and run. But I needed to focus. I was here for Paul.

I placed the bottle back in the rack as I returned to my reason for being there. "Paul said you organize wine auctions?"

"Just one, the Sonoma County Red Heart Charity auction, which happens every year. I also work as an importer."

"The Red Heart was where Paul bought the 1975 Chateau Clair Bleu, correct?"

"Yes, that's right."

I faced Henry, my back to the wines. "Do you know who sold that bottle? I mean, who put it up for auction?"

He looked surprised. "Why?"

I smiled. "Just curious. Since Paul enjoyed it so much."

Henry crossed his arms.

I suddenly felt the small space of the closet behind me and the image of Henry blocking my exit. I stepped past him into the hallway. "It meant so much for Paul to open that wine. And it's always fun to learn the wine's story. As a fellow wine lover, I'm sure you also like to know the history of every wine, especially those that come through your auction." I was rambling and I needed to tone it down a notch. I had to be calm and confident.

Henry slowly nodded. "I do. Although in this case, if I recall, the Chateau Clair Bleu was sold by a private party."

"Any chance you want to reveal the name of that private party?"

He tilted his head to the side as he studied me. "Katie, why are you really here?"

"I told you, the Mouton Rothschild. I think Paul wants to make sure you still have it. And as for my questions, I'm just curious about the auction. I'd love to know more about them in general." My game face was on, but I could feel it cracking under the anxiety that had taken hold of my lungs.

Henry's demeanor softened. He turned and removed the bottle of 1958 Chateau Mouton Rothschild from the shelf. "You can tell Paul you've confirmed I have it." The Dali designed label had a sheep drawn in curved lines with his signature in black ink on the left side. "You can also tell him that when, if ever, I decide to sell it, he'll be the first person I'll call."

"Thank you. I'll let him know."

Henry put the bottle back into its place in the wine rack. "As for the auction, the private party who sold the 1975 Chateau Clair Bleu would like to remain as such." Henry revealed a small smile and it was clear that sommeliers weren't the only wine industry workers who wore game faces.

My heart fell. I couldn't think of another way to get the information. "Do you get a lot of those? Anonymous private parties, I mean."

"Now and again. Often times it's someone wanting to sell their personal collection, but they don't want people to know."

I nodded. "Understood. Well, thanks for the information. This was helpful," I lied. I glanced at the bottles in the closet. "Thanks for showing me your collection. Especially the Chateau Margaux."

"You know, if you wanted to hang around for a little while, we could open the Margaux."

A spike of adrenaline shot through me. I could actually revisit the memory of that moment with my mother.

"I wouldn't mind sharing it with you," Henry said as he moved the hair off of my shoulder.

Maybe I hadn't read the situation wrong when I first came in. "Thank you for the offer, but it's time for me to leave." I walked up the stairs with Henry just a few steps behind me. "I'll let Paul know you still have the bottle and if I need anything else, Mr. Diven, I'll call you."

"Katie, I'm sorry," said Henry as he followed me to the front door. "You know, I didn't mean anything there. It was just a nice moment... that I ruined. I'm sorry."

I opened the front door and stood holding it as I turned to Henry. "It's fine, but I feel I should make it clear that I was here for Paul and only for Paul."

"I know and I'm sorry," said Henry, his face full of concern. "I felt connected to you right then. It's not often that I get a chance to talk with someone like you about things that I'm passionate about."

"Someone like me?"

"Nice, attractive, knowledgeable about wine. Again, I'm sorry. It was inappropriate and I was out of line."

The statement made me pause. I wasn't often called attractive. I didn't have a boyfriend and it wasn't a word that friends and family said in regular conversation. "Thank you, Mr. Diven. I must go." I stepped outside.

"Katie?"

I turned around.

Henry looked like a child who had been scolded. "Why do you really want to know the name of the private party?"

I hesitated. "I want to know the wine's journey. Where it was between the winery and now," I replied. "It meant a lot to Paul and I'd love to hear the story."

"Well, I can't give you the name of the private party who sold it at the auction, but I know who had it before they did. The previous owner. Would that help?"

"Who?"

"Roberto Morini."

"From Paul's dinner?"

"Yes. He has a wine shop on Pearl in Napa. Grand Vino. I don't think I'm crossing any privacy lines by telling you that the private party bought it from the shop a few months ago."

"Thank you." I headed down the steps.

"And Katie?"

I turned around once more.

"Are you working at Trentino this week?"

"Yes. Why?"

"Is it okay if I stop in? Purely as friends, of course."

I hesitated. "Mr. Diven—"

"Henry," he said.

"Henry," I replied, my expression emotionless, "you are free to do whatever you would like."

TEN

PAIRING SUGGESTION: CHÂTEAUNEUF-DU-PAPE

—CHÂTEAUNEUF-DU-PAPE, FRANCE

A red wine characterized by round stones, galets,
which surround the vines and retain the sun's heat into the night.

I DROVE TOWARD NAPA, passing the area where a truck had tried to force me off the road in the fall. Though my car was still damaged, I no longer feared being run off the road. The two people responsible were in prison. And now my focus was on wine and only on wine. One in particular and I had my next clue: Roberto's store.

I pressed my foot on the gas pedal as I flew into Napa Valley, not realizing how fast I was going until red and blue lights flashed in my rearview mirror. Great. A ticket.

I pulled over and waited as the squad car stopped behind me. This was going to be pricey. Paul said he would pay me to investigate, but I didn't know how much that would be and an expensive ticket was not what I needed.

I drummed my hands on the steering wheel as I waited for the officer to get out of the vehicle, give me a ticket, and possibly deliver a stern speech on how I was putting other lives at risk. I had received the lecture several times from my father, a police officer himself, even though I had only been ticketed once before. It was partly luck and partly because I usually drove the speed limit. But my mind was preoccupied today.

The officer finally got out of his car except he wasn't wearing the button-down beige uniform of a Napa Valley sheriff. Instead he had on a polo shirt with a logo over the left pocket area and khakis. And he had blond hair. And was tall.

A strange mixture of fear and excitement swelled through me. It could be him, and it could not be him.

The officer reached my window and there he was. Dean.

"Do you know how fast you were driving?" He leaned into the window and then stopped as his blue eyes met mine. "Katie?"

"Hi, Dean." I shifted uncomfortably in my seat. "It's nice to see you again."

"Yeah," he stumbled, clearly thrown off his routine. "What are you doing here?"

"Going to see a friend. He has a wine shop in downtown Napa."

"Oh," his voice lowered and I knew what he was thinking.

"Not that kind of friend. In fact, not really even a friend. It's more about business." Why was I constantly explaining myself? I stopped speaking and waited.

"Okay, well," said Dean. "You were speeding back there. Pretty fast, actually." He stepped back and motioned to the scrapes and dents that plagued the side doors. "You still haven't fixed this."

"No," I replied as I thought about what I could say. "I don't plan on it."

"Really?"

"I think the damage gives it character," I said, leaving out the fact that I really didn't have the money to fix it. "It makes it unique. We all have a little damage. It's what makes us, us. Like the vines that struggle, produce the best grapes—"

"If you keep driving like I just saw," Dean interrupted, the officer side of him taking over. Just like my father. "You're going to have more accidents."

"You know that one wasn't my fault." Although Dean hadn't been present when I was run off the road, it took place during a case we were both investigating. "I usually drive safely but I had a really good reason for speeding today." I cringed as I said it. As a cop's daughter, I should know better. My father would be furious if he knew I had been speeding.

"Try me." There was no smile, no twinkle in his eyes.

I didn't need to reiterate that I was going to Roberto's, so I tried a different tactic. "Maybe it was so I could get your attention."

"Really," he replied in a tone that didn't mean it. "You know, I called you."

"I know..."

"A few times." Dean put his hands in his pockets. "You never returned my calls."

"I know. I'm sorry. I was studying... I should have called you back."

"Well," said Dean. "What happened?"

"I don't know. It was the test and then work. I just never got around to calling—"

"That's not what I meant," he interrupted.

I looked at him, trying to think.

"Did you pass? Your test?"

"I did. I'm a Certified Sommelier now."

"Congratulations." Dean smiled, almost a pained smile, but it looked like he meant the compliment.

"Thank you."

Dean glanced at the cars passing us on the road. "Listen, I don't normally pull people over, I leave that to the patrol deputies, but your driving was unsafe. I don't want you to endanger others, or yourself . . . I've seen too many bad accidents along here. Too many fatalities."

"I know. I'm sorry," I replied. And I was. I looked up at Dean, his blond hair slicked back, his blue eyes brightly shining. He had been so nice to me and yet I had hurt him, even though I never meant to. "That's not all I'm sorry about," I said as I took a breath. "I should have called you back. I wanted to, but . . ." I paused. "I don't know. I'm complicated."

"Yeah, I learned that last fall." Dean stood up straighter and looked around. "Why the rush to get to a wine shop? Surely you have enough wine back in San Francisco."

"My mind was on something else."

"Such as?"

I hesitated.

Dean crossed his arms. "I thought we were past the secret keeping stage, Katie. Or do you still have more?"

"No, it's not that." I took a deep breath. "Yesterday Paul Rafferty's assistant Cooper—"

"Fell down the stairs," Dean interjected.

"Wait, how did you know?"

"I heard about it."

"It was terrible. He was at the base of the stairs when I found him. He was still alive but he passed away later."

Dean stared at me. "You were there?"

I nodded as I debated how much I should share with Dean. "But that's not all. Before Cooper died, we opened a bottle of wine Paul purchased at an auction. I think it was counterfeit."

"What do you mean?"

"I think it was a doctored bottle of wine. It was a new wine made to seem like it was from 1975. Anyway, I'm looking into it at the request of Paul Rafferty. He's paying me to find out who did it so he can go after them."

"Katie, didn't you learn last year that it isn't smart to get involved in these things? It's dangerous."

I stiffened in my seat. "Didn't you learn last year that because of me, Mark Plueger's murder was solved? The two people responsible are now locked away. Because of me."

Dean shook his head but his face broke into a smile. "You never change, Katie Stillwell."

"Some might say that's a good thing."

"I guess so," he said as he continued smiling. "Since you're working for Paul, does that mean you quit your job at Trentino?"

"No, I'm still doing that, too."

"Makes sense, since you've passed your test and you no longer need to study."

I started to grin and Dean noticed. "What?"

"I'm studying for my next test. The Advanced."

Dean looked down the road and back at me. "Well, you certainly like to keep busy."

I nodded.

"Listen, I don't really want to write you a ticket. Can you please slow down, keep it to the speed limit?"

"I will," I said with more excitement than I intended to display as I processed the thought of not receiving a ticket costing several hundred dollars. "I promise. Only the speed limit from now on."

"Good." He paused. "It was nice to see you again, Katie. Good luck with the Advanced and please drive safe." He started to walk away.

I opened my door and called to him. "Wait, Dean."

He took a few steps back toward my car.

"I really am sorry I didn't return your calls. If you call again, I'll answer." I paused. "I'd like you to call again."

Dean took a deep breath. "That's nice to hear." He glanced down at his watch. "Do you have some time before you go to the wine shop? I'm about to take my lunch break and I'd like to hear about this work for Paul Rafferty."

I stared at the road ahead, downtown Napa only a few minutes away. "I'd love to but I need to get to the store." I debated asking Dean to join me, but I needed to approach Roberto on my own first. "I want to make sure I have enough time there before I have to go to work."

Dean's face fell and my heart sank.

"But are you free tomorrow?" I added. "I can drive back up here."

Dean raised his eyebrows. "Are you sure?"

I nodded. "I'd really like to have lunch with you tomorrow."

Dean grinned. "Great. Where would you like to go? Or would you like me to recommend somewhere? There's a new sandwich shop in Yountville."

"Actually," I interjected as I thought about Alicia and Leanor's conversation at dinner. "Do you mind if we meet in Sonoma? There's a place that's been on my mind."

ELEVEN

An aromatic and traditionally unoaked Chardonnay,
though some houses are now starting to use oak.

જી

ROBERTO'S SHOP, GRAND VINO, was located on Main and Pearl in
the historic section of downtown Napa. It had a blue awning, large
windows, and a locked door. I pulled at the handle again to make
sure, but the door didn't budge.

I glanced at the sign in the window. OPEN TUESDAY THROUGH
SUNDAY. CLOSED MONDAYS. Great. I drove all the way to Napa for
nothing.

I leaned on the glass and put my hands around my face so I could
see in. Although it wasn't a large store, it was lined with bottles from
floor to ceiling and crates of wine formed aisles. But the store wasn't
completely absent of activity. There was a light on in the back.

I continued to look through the window, waiting for any sign of
movement. The level of light remained unchanged but that didn't

mean Roberto wasn't inside. It was worth giving it a full try before giving up.

I knocked on the glass. If someone on the street saw me, they might think I was breaking in and call the cops. Hopefully the responding officer would be Dean.

A gentleman moved out of the shadows and into the light.

I tapped on the window.

He stepped closer. It was Roberto. He waved his hand horizontally, to signify that the shop was closed.

I nodded and tapped again.

Roberto, with a clear look of frustration on his face, came to the front door and unlocked it, only opening it a few inches. "We're closed today," his accent clipped.

"Roberto, it's me. Katie Stillwell. From last night."

Roberto's face lit up and he opened the door wide. "Katherine, come in, come in. What are you doing here?"

I stepped into the store, a smile forming as I did. I loved being around all of the bottles of wine, knowing each one was waiting for their moment to shine. But as much as I wanted to see the wines Roberto had for sale, I had to focus on my reason for being there. I also needed to decide how I was going to play this. "I thought it might be nice to stop by."

"I'm glad you came to visit," said Roberto as he moved behind the counter that had four leather bar stools in front. "I do inventory on Mondays. I was about to leave so you caught me right on time. Here, take a seat."

"Oh, I don't need to sit. I won't be here long."

"No, sit down. You're my guest." Roberto's face lit up with his huge smile. "It's wine time. What can I pour for you?"

I pulled up a bar stool and sat down. "Well, I'm actually not here for that."

"Nonsense. That's not how we work around here." He grabbed a glass and placed it in front of me. "Red or white?"

I stared at the empty glass and then shifted my focus to him. "Surprise me."

Roberto's eyes glistened and he turned to the fridge behind him. "What brings you to the area? I thought you were based in San Francisco."

"I'm working on something with Paul."

"Oh?" The sound of bottles being moved around filled the air. "It was so sad that Cooper fell down the stairs." He brought out a bottle. "Are you his new assistant? Taking over for Cooper?"

An interesting deduction, but I decided not to comment. "No, not exactly. I work at Trentino."

"What do you do at Trentino?"

"I'm a sommelier."

Roberto flashed a smile. "Now it makes sense, Katherine. You knew a lot about wine last night." He poured a white wine into the glass, the label turned away from me. "Here you go. I brought a case of this in last week. It's amazing. Like blow-your-mind great." He motioned with his hands exploding near his head.

"What is it?"

He laughed. "I'm not going to tell you. I want your opinion first."

I swirled the wine and took a deep sniff, a heavy scent of lychee floating from the glass. I sipped. The wine was well-balanced with almost a limestone quality to it. There was grapefruit and lychee, along with strong minerality. My mind raced to identify the wine. Possible varietals included Gewürztraminer, Pinot Blanc, and Riesling.

"Do you like it, Katherine?"

I nodded, an unavoidable smile on my face. "It's beautiful."

Roberto reached for the bottle. "Yes, it's a—"

"No," I interrupted.

He raised his eyebrows.

"Let me figure it out." I took another sip, which confirmed my deduction. "It's an Alsatian Gewürztraminer. Gotta love that lychee."

Roberto turned the bottle to reveal the label of a Gewürztraminer from Alsace. "I'm impressed."

I wanted to say that they didn't call me The Palate for nothing, but I kept quiet.

"Let me pour you another one."

My eyes flicked to the bottles behind him before shaking my head. "No, that's not why I'm here."

"That's right. Paul. Is he looking for a specific bottle?"

My mind raced to think of a question before diving into the Chateau Clair Bleu. "He's interested in Mouton Rothschilds."

"Wonderful. I have a few of them over here." Roberto walked over to a glass case and pointed to three bottles of Mouton Rothschild. "What year did he want?"

I stood up from the stool and followed him to the glass case. None of the bottles were from 1958.

"Not sure," I replied. "But if he wanted to get different years, would you be able to order them?"

"Of course." Roberto returned to the bar and I sank back onto the stool.

"What about another Chateau Clair Bleu?"

Roberto nodded. "We have two in the store."

"Are either of them a 1975?"

"Like the one we opened last night? No, sadly."

"You sold that bottle, correct?"

Roberto studied me for a moment. "Paul bought that wine at the Red Heart Auction, I believe. I don't sell wine at auctions. My focus is here at the store." Roberto motioned around at the bottles lining the walls.

"But you had the wine before then, didn't you? I heard it came from your shop. Not directly before the auction, but a few months ago, right?"

Roberto's smile faded. "Katherine, I'm sorry, but you're mistaken. I never owned the bottle."

"I must have heard it incorrectly," I replied. If Roberto didn't trust me, that was one thing. But if he was telling the truth, that was another problem altogether. I needed to soften the mood. "Paul seems like a great guy. I'm glad to be helping him with his wine collection."

Roberto poured himself a pale red wine, most likely a Pinot Noir, and sat down across from me. "One of the best."

"You know him pretty well, right?"

"Paul and I go back a long time. Probably before you were even born."

I faked a grin. I hated when people said things like that. It threw an immediate undercurrent into the conversation, like they were staking a claim that I would never know as much as them. Perhaps I was just being oversensitive, but I didn't like to be thought of as young and naive.

Roberto took a sip of his wine. "I met Paul back in New York and we've been friends ever since."

"And you're just friends?"

"Are you implying that Paul and I are romantically involved?"

"No, nothing like that. I mean, sorry," I tripped over my words. I took a deep breath and started again. "What I mean is, have you ever worked together?"

"Worked together? I don't understand. I'm in wine, he's in law."

"But he's bought bottles here?" I pointed to the shelves around us.

"Yes, he's been a devoted customer for many years." Roberto looked down at his glass.

"Did you know he was a fan of Chateau Clair Bleu?"

"Of course. We've discussed wine at length over the years."

"Did you know he'd always wanted a 1975?"

Roberto laughed. "I think all of his friends did."

"It's a shame that you weren't able to get it for him."

Roberto shook his head. "If I had one, I would have brought it to Paul's attention." He stared at me. "What is this all about, Katherine? Is Paul asking you to ask me?" He frowned. "I know Paul well enough that if he has a question, he can call me himself."

I shook my head. "No, not at all. It's just that I'm helping him build his wine collection and I want to make sure this is a store where I can find rare bottles."

Roberto relaxed and took another sip of his wine. "Of course. I will do my best to get any bottle you or Paul desire." He motioned to his glass. "I'm not a fan of drinking alone. What can I open for you?"

"Thank you but I should go." I smiled at him. "I have to drive back to the city."

He looked at his watch. "In fact, it's time for me to get going as well. I'll just put the inventory book away in the back."

"Book? You do your inventory by hand? Isn't it easier to do it on the computer?"

"Old habits die hard," said Roberto. "I've owned wine shops for twenty years. My son tried to get me to switch over to computer records, but I love the paper trail."

I thought of my paper flash cards instead of digital ones and nodded. "Thanks for letting me in the store, even though it was closed. It was great to chat with you."

"My pleasure. Don't be a stranger, Katherine." He winked but it made me uncomfortable. There was some element to him that I didn't trust. He was a salesman, always selling something to someone. I didn't want to be the gullible one. Roberto denied having the Chateau Clair Bleu in the store, but Henry told me he had. One of them was lying, I just didn't know which one.

TWELVE

PAIRING SUGGESTION: PROSECCO—VENETO, ITALY

A sparkling wine aged with less pressure than Champagne,
resulting in lighter bubbles.

❧

WHEN I ARRIVED BACK at my apartment, I immediately set off for my run through Golden Gate Park. I usually ran in the morning, but right now I needed to clear my head before I went to work. I thought about Henry's mention of Roberto previously owning the bottle and Roberto denying it. There had to be a reason for one of them to lie and I wanted to know what it was.

My normal running path through the length of the park didn't seem like the right choice today. Maybe it was time to switch things up. See things from a different perspective. I turned at Stow Lake and started running north, heading into the streets.

I had to dodge more people, but the different route was a welcome change. I passed coffee shops where I would like to sit in the future, a few restaurants I might like to try, and some stores I would probably venture into at some point after I was financially stable again.

I continued through the streets and started the climb into the Presidio, a former military base and now a park. With every turn I made, my feelings about the situation became clear. I needed to talk to Henry again, or to Roberto, or both.

Deep breaths filled my lungs as my legs pumped toward the Golden Gate Bridge, the red posts in the distance closer with every stride. I should have stopped and turned around, but I didn't want to. Like my goal to become a Master Sommelier, I wasn't going to give up. My sights were set on the red posts, just like the red Master Sommelier pin I would achieve one day. I wouldn't give up on that and I wouldn't give up on my task for Paul, to find out the origin of the 1975 Chateau Clair Bleu.

I could easily tell Paul about Roberto and Henry, but that wasn't getting to the heart of the issue. I said I would figure out the name of the counterfeiter for Paul and at this point, I either had two possibilities or two clues.

The bridge was beneath me now, the San Francisco Bay below. Built in 1937, the bridge connects San Francisco to Marin and although I had biked across it with Kurt, I had never run over it before. I maneuvered past people walking and biking as the traffic roared to my left. The length of the bridge was over a mile and half and I had already run longer than my usual routine, but I kept going.

The ocean breeze was cold, but once I passed the midpoint, I didn't see a reason to stop.

Could Roberto have counterfeited the wine and then sold it? I needed to find out if it had been in his store. If not, I would go back to Henry but I would rather talk more to Roberto first. Eliminate possibilities, or in this case, perhaps find the one I needed.

I was on solid ground again and my legs pumped up the slight incline as the city of San Francisco rose to my right across the bay.

My muscles burned and I slowed my pace, arriving at the Vista Point where tourists often stop to take pictures of the city after crossing the bridge. It was a clear day, free of the fog.

I took deep breaths, my lungs aching from the extra effort and distance. When I had calmed my breathing, I stared at the city I had called my home for the last four years. Although it had its downsides, as everywhere did, it was a great place to live and I was happy to be there. A beautiful city full of culture and romance and only an hour from wine country. I wanted to stay there, which meant I needed to figure out my financial situation. And I would. By solving the problem for Paul.

"Katie?"

I turned around. Someone was waving from a black Mercedes Sedan in the parking lot. I stepped closer but still couldn't recognize them. They knew my name so maybe it was a customer from Trentino.

I took a few more slow steps toward the waving figure in the car until I could see his shiny bald head. It was Simon, a guest from the dinner at Paul's house.

"Oh, hey Simon."

"I thought that was you." The car was still running.

"You knew it was me in this huge parking lot?" I put my hands on my knees and took a deep breath. My lungs had tightened and I felt myself straining for a full breath.

"I was just leaving and I drove by. It looked like you so I figured I would stop and say hi. Sorry, I didn't mean to disturb your run. I only called out 'cause I thought you were done."

I glanced around. "No, it's fine. I'm finished. I don't usually run this far."

"Do you live around here?"

"No, I live by Golden Gate Park. I can't believe I ran all this way." It must have been close to seven miles. I would be hurting tomorrow.

"Here." He leaned over and opened the door. "I'm heading that way. I'll give you a lift."

"Thank you, but I should walk. I'm pretty sweaty."

"It's up to you, but I don't mind. I can drive with the windows down."

I laughed as I looked across the bay. It would take me a long time to walk back to my apartment and I needed to get to work.

"Actually, that would be great." I went around and climbed into the car. It smelled like vanilla though there wasn't a noticeable air freshener. "What were you doing at the Vista Point?"

Simon pulled out of the parking lot. "I have to drop something off in the city for work, but I like to stop and take in the view on my way in. Enjoying the little things in life, you know?"

"What do you do for work?"

"A little of this, a little of that."

"That's pretty vague."

Simon laughed. "That's what Leanor says, too."

He dodged the work question but I still wanted to know. "So what do you do?"

A small smile grew on Simon's face. "I work for a private company that deals with mergers and acquisitions. And you? What do you do, Katie?"

"I'm a sommelier at Trentino." I waited, unsure if I could trust Simon, but I needed to find out more information. "But right now I'm helping Paul with his wine cellar. Earlier I went to Grand Vino."

Simon smiled. "Roberto's store."

"Have you shopped there?"

He shrugged. "Maybe once. I'm not sure."

"Do you know Roberto pretty well?"

He glanced at me. "Why, are you interested in him? I'm sure I can set you two up on a date, but he doesn't seem like your type."

I laughed. "No, it's not that. I was just wondering if I should build more of Paul's collection from his store." His earlier comment dawned on me. "And wait, what's my type?"

"I don't know. Someone very down to earth. Except Leanor said you'd probably like someone with money."

"You and Leanor talked about me?"

Simon shrugged again. "Leanor talks about everyone."

His comments rolled over in my mind. "Does Roberto not have a lot of money then?"

Simon grinned. "So Leanor was right."

"No, just curious." If Roberto was in a difficult financial situation, the money from counterfeit wine would give him a way out of it. But if he did have the Clair Bleu, why not sell it to Paul right away since he knew he wanted it?

"But seriously," Simon continued. "If you're interested in Roberto, you should know a few things about him."

"Such as?"

"Well, he's been married." Simon tapped the wheel.

"Okay."

"And he's super devoted to his work."

"Seriously? Not an issue," I replied.

"But he's a good guy. Always plays by the book."

I glanced at Simon. "Interesting. What about Henry Diven?"

"He's single and actively looking."

"I gathered."

"Yeah, I've heard he can be rather forward. However"—Simon looked at me—"if you're really interested in one of them, you should talk to Alicia Trager. She's known both of them for years."

"I might do that." I motioned ahead and gave Simon directions as we got closer to the park.

"I bet you open a lot of great wines at Trentino."

"I do."

"You know, if you ever open any older bottles from Bordeaux or Burgundy, I know Alicia would be interested."

"What do you mean?"

"She likes to collect the labels and make them into tiles. You should see their kitchen. It's pretty impressive."

"Thanks," I said as I thought about the bottle of 1990 Gevrey-Chambertin, Clos Saint-Jacques, an expensive Burgundy I had opened for a table on Friday. They had finished the wine and since they left the empty bottle, Bill decided to keep it on display near the time clock. Or at least it was during my last shift on Saturday. My mind suddenly focused. Why was Simon telling me this? "Would she want to buy them from me?" I asked.

"I don't know about that, but since you said you might talk to her about your new love interest"—Simon winked—"it would be helpful to have something she's interested in. That's all I'm saying." There was more to Simon's comment, but I couldn't read it.

I realized the car had stopped and Simon was waiting for more directions.

"I'm the third street on the right."

Simon turned and I pointed to the two-story Art Deco apartment building. "I'm over here."

"Are you going to Trentino now?"

I opened the door. "Yes. In a bit."

"Leanor and I should come in some time."

"I agree. Maybe tomorrow ..." I paused, debating how to approach it. I decided to feign surprise. "Oh, wait. Aren't Leanor and Alicia meeting for lunch in Sonoma tomorrow?"

Simon shrugged. "Possibly. I can't keep up with her schedule."

"Aren't you two married?"

"Me and Leanor?" Simon laughed. "No, we've just known each other a very long time. You could say we nearly have a common law marriage, but it's not even that. We're like best friends and worst enemies all in one. It's very complicated."

I smiled. "Isn't everything in life?"

"I guess it is," Simon replied, but his focus was on the street in front of him.

I stepped out of the car. "Thanks again for the ride. I appreciate it."

He turned to me. "You're welcome."

I started to shut the door, but Simon put his hand up like he wanted to say something. "Katie?"

I held the door and waited. "Yes."

"Whatever you're doing, or whatever you're going to do, please be careful."

"Thanks." I smiled and closed the door, but Simon's comment stayed with me as I climbed the stairs to my apartment. I already had my suspicions about Simon, suddenly being where I was across the bay where neither of us lived, and now with what seemed like a helpful warning. I didn't know what he meant, but I wasn't going to dismiss it. I needed to pay attention to all of the clues, including ones about my safety.

I would pick up the empty bottle of 1990 Gevrey-Chambertin at Trentino during my shift in case I saw Alicia tomorrow. I didn't know if I would need it, but just like going into the Advanced Exam, it was best to be fully prepared.

THIRTEEN

PAIRING SUGGESTION: PINOT GRIS—WILLAMETTE VALLEY, OREGON

*Oregon's most widely grown white grape produces
flavors of peach and nectarine.*

❧

BILL WAS STANDING NEXT to the bar at Trentino that evening, the same great smile on his face as always. "Feeling okay? Your cheeks are a little pink," he said.

"Fine, still recovering from a long run. Hey, you know the 1990 Gevrey-Chambertin, Clos Saint-Jacques I opened on Friday? Do we still have it?"

"Of course. It's on the sideboard by the time clock."

Bill followed me as I walked down the hall. There was the bottle, its label perfectly preserved as if it still held the secrets and magic of the Pinot Noir that used to be inside.

I picked up the bottle and held it. "Are you planning on doing anything with it?"

"Well," said Bill, "I thought it looked pretty nice adorning the clock." He winked. "What's this about?"

"I thought I might offer it to a friend."

"Is this a romantic gesture for someone?"

"Ha, no. Not at all." I debated for a few seconds. "Bill, can I confide in you for a moment? Do you have time?"

"Katie, I always have time for you."

I shared with him that the 1975 Chateau Clair Bleu was a fake.

Bill kept shaking his head as I told him the details.

"I can't believe it. After all that money and for Paul to open it at a special dinner. Devastating to be cheated like that."

"Then Cooper's death."

"The poor guy." Bill looked at me. "But I'm proud of you for figuring it out. I can't say I'm surprised. The Palate in full force."

"But I kind of broke the sommelier rule, the one when someone is enjoying a bottle of wine they bought and don't know it's corked or spoiled. I told Paul it was counterfeit. Not at the dinner, because that ended when Cooper fell down the stairs. But here, earlier. I felt he needed to know."

"I don't think you were wrong to tell him. He deserved to know. Especially after he paid that much for it."

"Well, Paul's hired me to look into who counterfeited the wine." I waited for Bill to tell me that I shouldn't be doing it, for me to be careful, to not get involved.

"Where will you start?"

I paused. "Really?"

Bill nodded. "Have you checked who the seller was at the auction?"

"It was a private party, but I found out that the bottle used to be at a wine shop in Napa."

Bill opened his mouth to talk but I continued before he had a chance. "I've already been to the wine shop but he denied ever having it. I'm following up on it tomorrow."

"With the bottle?"

"No, actually that's just in case I get the opportunity to talk to someone who might know more."

Bill tilted his head. "Okay. So how are you going to follow up on it?"

"Not sure yet. Either get him to admit he owned the wine without putting myself in danger, or go back to the person who told me he did."

"Let me know if you need any help," said Bill.

I smiled as an idea dawned on me about how to handle Roberto tomorrow with a little help from an old friend. I looked at the Gevrey-Chambertin. "So can I take this after my shift tonight?"

"Of course. You opened the bottle, you served it, and the guest didn't want to keep it. I would say it's yours to do with what you like."

"Thanks." I glanced at the bottle, wishing it was still filled with wine.

"Will you be back from Napa in time for work tomorrow? Although I know Paul is great and I'm sure he's paying for you, I don't want to lose you as my sommelier."

"Bill, my number-one dedication is to Trentino."

Bill shook his head. "I disagree."

"What?"

"Your number-one dedication is to studying for your Advanced Exam this fall."

"Oh," I replied. "Right."

"You're not studying, are you?"

I tapped my fingers on the bottle and outlined the label with my thumb. "Soon."

"Katie, you've got to keep on it. Don't let distractions keep from you achieving your dream."

"It's just a short break. To help Paul."

"There will always be diversions. Always. If you let every single distraction slow you down, you'll never get to the next level. That test will be here before you know it."

I stood up straighter and put my shoulders back. "I'll be ready." I knew Bill was right. I needed to learn to balance it all. I would get back to studying. But before that, I had to call an old friend to help me tomorrow. A friend who was great at distractions.

FOURTEEN

PAIRING SUGGESTION: NERO D'AVOLA—SICILY, ITALY

*A red wine with strong tannins and similarities
to Cabernet Sauvignon and Syrah.*

TESSA WAS WAITING FOR me when I arrived outside Roberto's wine shop on Tuesday morning. Ever since she became second in charge at Frontier Winery, she had toned down her clothing from her former revealing style. Her dark gray dress had a high neck but she still wore four-inch heels. Some things about Tessa would never change.

"Thanks for coming," I said as I hugged her.

"Are you kidding? A secret mission to find out about a fake wine? I wouldn't miss this for the *world*." She laughed and flipped her blond hair to the side. "Besides, Roberto is fun. I've met him a few times."

"That's perfect. Just keep him busy." I took a breath. "Ready?"

"Always."

We entered Grand Vino, which was quiet, having only been open for thirty minutes.

"Katherine, welcome back," said Roberto as we approached the counter. "And Tessa!" His Italian accent emphasized the sound of her name. "Are you bringing me a case of Frontier?" He raised his eyebrows as he looked at Tessa. Frontier Winery produced wine known as being exclusive, high quality, and only sold through their wine club and a few high-end restaurants.

"Maybe," said Tessa with a grin. She sat down on the barstool. "What are we tasting today, Roberto?"

"I just received a case of Nero d'Avola that I know you'll both love. In fact, it will blow your mind," Roberto replied, repeating the same expression as the day before. "I have a bottle open for tasting. Would you like to try it?"

"*Assolutamente!*" replied Tessa.

Roberto's face lit up. "Tessa! You speak Italian?"

"No." She winked.

This was my chance. "Roberto, do you mind if I use the restroom?"

"Not at all. It's through the rear hallway, second door."

"Thanks, I'll just be a moment." I headed to the back room and glanced around. There wasn't anything of note at first, but on the shelf, next to the bathroom door, was a line of log books. Each one had the word INVENTORY followed by the year.

I grabbed the book from 2016 and started flipping through the pages, looking for the Chateau Clair Bleu. A rush of adrenaline pumped through me when I saw a mention of Chateau Clair Bleu, but the year was 1993. I continued to turn the pages while keeping an ear on Tessa and Roberto's conversation, which had shifted to the new sushi restaurant in town.

I flicked through page after page as my heart raced. I only had a minute, if that. Tessa was ideal at distractions but eventually Roberto would realize I was missing.

I turned to the next page and there it was, a 1975 Chateau Clair Bleu, brought into inventory in September. Roberto had been in possession of the wine after all.

I flushed the toilet in the bathroom so my reason to go back there seemed legitimate and then rejoined Roberto and Tessa in the front of the store.

"Katherine, there you are. I thought maybe you got lost." He pushed an empty glass toward me and poured a tasting of the Nero d'Avola. "Enjoy."

"Thanks," I replied as I picked it up. My hand shook and I hoped he didn't notice. I swirled, the red wine climbing the sides of the glass, and took a sip.

"Apparently it's Roberto's favorite," said Tessa, and she mimicked her hands exploding near her head.

He laughed but I knew I had to get to the point.

"Roberto, I need to talk to you." I paused as I shifted my direction on how to broach the subject. "I want you to know that I know."

He raised his eyebrows. "Know what?"

"That you had the 1975 Chateau Clair Bleu in your store. The one that Paul bought. You denied it yesterday, but what I want to know is why?"

"How do you know I had it in the store?"

I put my game face on. I decided to proceed and keep control of the conversation. "I'm curious why you didn't tell Paul that you had it in stock when you did. Knowing that he had always wanted a 1975 Chateau Clair Bleu."

Roberto's gaze fell to the counter and he didn't move.

"Is it because you knew it was fake?"

He looked up at me. "It's fake?"

"Just like Katie's hair color," said Tessa.

I ignored her and proceeded. "You didn't know when you tasted the wine at the dinner?"

Color flooded into Roberto's face. "I was still recovering from a cold. I couldn't properly smell or taste anything." He looked at me. "Katherine, how did you know?"

"I could tell. It wasn't how a 1975 Chateau Clair Bleu should be. It was fruit forward and not representative of the region."

Tessa nudged me with her elbow. "See. The Palate."

I smiled but returned my focus to Roberto. "Well, I'm relieved you didn't know, but I still don't understand one thing. Why did you lie to me yesterday?"

"It's complicated, Katherine. You said you were working for Paul. I didn't want you to tell him the bottle had been in my store. He would have wondered why I didn't sell it to him."

"Why didn't you? If you'd known for years that he'd wanted it, why not just call him up?"

Roberto shook his head. "I honestly forgot when it arrived. I have a lot of bottles coming in and out of here. By the time I remembered, it had already sold."

"So..." I waited for Roberto to jump in.

"So," said Tessa instead. "Where did it come from?" she asked, her glass now empty.

"The Nero?"

Tessa gave him a look. "Please. The Chateau Clair Bleu."

Roberto took a deep breath. "I don't know off the top of my head."

"Can you look?" I asked.

"Why?"

"Paul wants to know. He wants to follow through on it. He wants to find out who made it."

Roberto nodded. "But Katherine, how did you know it was here?"

"I heard it from a friend." I kept my expression neutral. Henry wasn't exactly a friend, but he had steered me in the right direction. "Listen, this is all to help Paul. He wants to proceed with finding who created it. It won't involve you."

Roberto nodded. "Come on to the back."

"This is fun," remarked Tessa.

"Seriously, Tessa?"

"Listen, we don't investigate counterfeit bottles of wine at the winery. You have an exciting life."

I thought back to my empty studio apartment. "Not really."

Roberto pulled out the inventory book I had looked at only moments earlier and flipped through the pages until he stopped at the one with the Chateau Clair Bleu. "Sorry, it's not going to be as easy as you hoped."

"What do you mean?"

Roberto pointed to the page. "I had my son help me with inventory for a few months. He didn't write down the initials of where the bottles came from. The Chateau Clair Bleu was during that time."

I stepped forward and looked at the page. Roberto had lied to me at first, about owning the bottle, but this time he was truthful. The column on the left was blank on the entire page and for the next few pages.

"But it was only last year. Surely you would know who it was."

He shook his head. "So many bottles come into this store. I don't remember." He glanced at the boxes behind him. "But I can find out. It'll be on the purchase order."

I looked at the pages flowing out of the boxes without any form of organization. "Will that take a long time?"

"Maybe," replied Roberto. "I can phone you as soon I find it."

"Perfect." I wrote down my number on a card and handed it to him. "Thank you, Roberto."

"My pleasure, Katherine."

Tessa linked arms with me and we left the store, heading toward our cars.

"Want to grab lunch?" she asked.

"I can't. I'm meeting Dean."

"Shut the front door. You're kidding."

"I'm not."

Tessa grinned. "Lucky girl. Details later?"

"It's not a date. It's just getting together as friends."

"Sure. Enjoy your lunch," said Tessa, with air quotes around the word *lunch*. She motioned to the dents on my car. "And get that fixed."

"Working on it."

FIFTEEN

PAIRING SUGGESTION: BLANC DE BLANCS CHAMPAGNE

—REIMS, FRANCE

*Made from 100% Chardonnay, this wine ages well
and pairs with most meals and situations.*

❧

DEAN WAS STANDING NEXT to his car when I pulled into the parking lot of the Fremont Diner. It was a popular spot just inside Sonoma, with a rusty old truck in the corner as a permanent welcoming accessory and the menu written on a large chalkboard.

"I was worried you wouldn't show up," said Dean as I greeted him.

"Really?"

He shrugged. "I don't know. I thought you would've returned my calls in the fall and you didn't. You're an enigma, Katie. But I'm glad you're here."

"I'm glad I'm here, too. Have you been to the Fremont before?"

"Once," said Dean. "A buddy of mine works not far away at the Monument Hotel. We grabbed lunch here one time."

I stared at the large menu on the wall above the cash register. Although the Fremont Diner was known for a variety of meals, my favorite was the fried chicken on top of a crispy waffle.

"I think I'll go for a burger," said Dean.

"Chicken and waffles for me," I replied.

Dean paid for both our meals even though I politely refused his offer at first.

We took a seat at one of the blue picnic benches in the fenced-off garden while we waited for our number to be called.

"So," Dean said with a sense of hesitation. "Mind if I address the elephant in the room?"

I glanced around at our outdoor setting and raised my eyebrows.

"Well, the elephant in the garden."

This was going to be about not calling him back. I took a deep breath. "You want to know ..."

"About the test." He motioned with his hand. "Yesterday, you said you passed. Tell me more about it."

I grinned as the memory came to mind. "I actually ended up with the highest score. They only call out the names of those who pass so I was pretty nervous and nearly jumped when they called out my name last."

"How was the blind tasting this time?"

"Really great. I made clear calls and didn't waver once."

"I can't say I'm surprised. Katie, I'm really proud of you." He stared right into my eyes as he said it and my stomach flipped.

"Thank you."

Dean smiled. "So what happens now? With your studying, I mean. You said something yesterday about the next one?"

"Yeah, it continues. I'm going for the Advanced later this year."

"And then after the Advanced?"

"I'll start studying for the Master's exam. But you have to be invited to take that test. You can't just apply."

"Number forty-two," said a voice over the loud speaker.

"I'll get it, just a sec." Dean stood up from the table and returned a moment later with our food. "What would you pair with that?" He motioned to my chicken and waffles.

"Champagne. It goes well with salty food and happens to be perfect with fried chicken."

"Well, I think it would go well with anything. I wish we had some. We could celebrate your test."

"Thanks." I felt my cheeks twinge with heat so I focused on my meal, uncomfortable at the camaraderie that was between us. Not the fact that it was happening, but that I had pushed him away before.

"And studying for the Master's exam, that can take years, right?"

"How do you know that?"

Dean smiled. "I did some research yesterday while I looked forward to this lunch." He picked up his burger. "I wanted to see how long it would be until you returned another one of my calls. Looks like it'll be a few years." He took a bite.

"No." I cut a piece of the chicken, a thin layer of syrup covering it. "I wouldn't say that." I started eating while Dean waited with an inquisitive look on his face. "If you call again, I promise I'll call you back," I added.

"Sure."

"No, I mean it. I like having you around."

Dean's eyes twinkled. "I'm glad."

"And you? How is work going?"

"It's going well. Putting the bad guys away, you know. I like knowing I'm making a difference."

"I like that you do that." I smiled and he winked.

"Me too," he replied.

We ate for a few moments in silence.

"So the chicken and waffles, they're pretty good? Is that why you wanted to come here?"

"This place was mentioned at the dinner I attended on Sunday. Paul's dinner. I thought it would be fun to eat here." I glanced around. "Also, two of the people from that night said they might be eating here today."

"Are they?"

I glanced around at the rest of the tables. "No. But I figured it was a long shot anyway. I mean, they were coming today but who knows what time. It would be a coincidence if they were here right now."

"You know I don't really believe in coincidences."

I smiled. "Neither do I. It's funny because I actually brought a bottle for one of them just in case, but I don't think I need it anymore."

"That reminds me," said Dean. "Yesterday you alluded that you were working for Paul. Looking into a wine?"

"Oh, that. Well ..." I paused. "I'm almost done. I've nearly found out where it came from. Just a little more investigating to do."

"Will it be dangerous?"

"I don't think so. But you know that's not going to stop me."

"Yeah," Dean said as his voice dropped. "I know." He took another bite of his burger. After a moment, he said, "So what will you do once you know where it's from?"

"Tell Paul." I shrugged. "What else did you expect?" I grinned at Dean. "Lighten up, I'll be fine. I've tracked it down to a wine shop and the owner is getting me the name of where it came from and then I'll give that to Paul and be done. He's going to pursue the rest legally. I'm only figuring out the name."

I touched his hand and Dean visibly reacted in a way that he was clearly surprised. "I promise I'll be careful."

He nodded. "What if the shop owner doesn't give you the name?"

A movement to Dean's left made me turn. Two people, each carrying a tray of food, sat down a few tables away. Leanor and Alicia.

"Dean, you know how you don't believe in coincidences? The two people I mentioned just sat down."

"You're kidding."

"No, see them there?" I motioned my head to three tables away. "That's Leanor and Alicia." My mind started to turn. "Actually, if you'll excuse me for a moment, I want to go say hi."

"I didn't get the impression that you were friends with them."

"I'm not." I smiled. "But you made a really good point. If Roberto, the wine shop owner, doesn't come back with the name, I'll need to explore other avenues. I'll be right back."

"I'll be here," Dean replied.

I put on a polite smile as I approached their table.

Alicia was the first to look up. "Katie? Lovely to see you again so soon."

"Sonoma's a small town after all," added Leanor.

"Are you dining alone?" asked Alicia. "Would you like to join us?"

"Ah, no, thanks. I'm having lunch with a friend." I motioned back to Dean, who waved. "Have you talked to Paul?"

"Poor chap. He's really distraught over the death of Cooper, as we all are," said Alicia. "I might stop by there later today to see how he's doing."

"You've known him a long time, right?"

Alicia glanced at Leanor before answering. "I've known him about ten years, when I married Martin. They're best friends. Leanor, you've known him about five, I think?"

"Six," she replied dryly.

"What about Roberto?"

"We've met Roberto many times," said Leanor. "In fact, the only person we didn't know at the dinner was you." She started eating but Alicia kept her attention on me.

"Alicia, you're good friends with him, right?"

"Katie," said Leanor. "For someone standing in front of two people who are trying to eat"—she motioned to her food—"you ask a lot of questions."

"Sorry. I didn't mean to interrupt your lunch. I have food waiting on the table over there, too."

"Then you should go eat it," said Leanor with a half smile on her face, as if she were trying to be polite, but not really.

"You're absolutely right." I smiled and took a step back. "One last question. Alicia, I heard you liked the labels off of old wine bottles."

"Who told you that?"

"Simon."

"Simon?" Alicia locked eyes with Leanor, who kept the same dry expression on her face.

"When did you see Watkins?" asked Leanor.

"Yesterday in the city." There was a notable tension to the air and I didn't like it. "I have an empty bottle of 1990 Gevrey-Chambertin, Clos Saint-Jacques. Might you be interested in it?"

Alicia rubbed her lips together and looked up to the sky before returning her focus to me. "Yes, I'd love to see it. Why don't you bring it by the house later today? I live off of Boyes Boulevard. Do you know the area?"

I nodded even though I wasn't sure. That was a convenient thing about cell phones, I could look up anything.

Alicia gave me the address. "Stop by after you're done here. I have some shopping to do but I'll be there."

Leanor smiled again. "Nice to see you again, Katie. Let's keep in touch," she said in a voice that meant anything but that. I knew it was my cue to leave and I thanked them and stepped away, but Leanor's tone continued to go through my head. She didn't like me, that was clear, and I wanted to know why.

SIXTEEN

PAIRING SUGGESTION: CABERNET FRANC

—SIERRA FOOTHILLS, CALIFORNIA

This red wine has higher alcohol than its Cabernet Franc
counterparts grown in other regions.

☙

When I arrived back at the table, Dean had already finished his burger. I sat down and took a bite of my chicken and waffles. They were cold. I ate them anyway, cutting small slices of each as my mind turned.

"Find out anything helpful?" asked Dean when I had eaten the last piece of cold chicken.

I shook my head. "Not really. I mean, I'm already all set in my investigation, but it's always good to keep an eye out for clues." I motioned to Leanor. "But she doesn't like me. That's a clue. She didn't like it when I said I had talked with her husband yesterday. Or not her husband. Her boyfriend, I guess."

"Why do you think that's a clue?" Dean tilted his head to the side. "It could be something else."

I leaned back on the bench. "What do you mean?"

"Listen, I don't know anything about what went on over there and what was said, but I know how you smile. If she thought that's how you were with him, she might be feeling threatened. Maybe she's protective of her husband."

"He's not her husband."

"Or whatever he is. I'm just letting you know."

"Can't a girl talk to a guy without someone getting jealous? Sometimes we're just talking to people."

Dean put his hands in front of him. "I'm only saying what I saw."

"You got jealous when I was talking to Jeff last fall."

"And he turned out to be a bad guy." Dean smiled.

"Okay, okay. But listen, I'll be careful. Around everyone." I motioned to Alicia and Leanor, who had stood up, already finished with their meal.

"Good," replied Dean. "Now let's talk about wine instead. I had a bottle of Pinot Noir from Santa Rita Hills this week. It was really nice."

"I'm glad you liked it. The region is beautiful. I haven't been there in a while but I should visit again."

"There's the Katie I remember." He winked.

"What do you mean?"

"Anytime we talk about wine, your face lights up. Wine makes you happy. I like seeing you happy."

"Thanks." I looked at our empty plates. "Thanks for having lunch with me. This was fun. We should do it again."

"Yeah?" Dean looked surprised.

"Yeah," I replied.

"Are you heading back to the city now? Work tonight?"

"Yes, but I'm going to Alicia's house first. She said I could stop by there after this and show her the bottle."

"Be careful."

"I will."

Dean glanced at his car and back at me. "I wish I could come with you."

"You'd want to come with me?"

"Of course." He smiled and my stomach leapt. "So if I call you later, will you answer?"

"Definitely."

———

When I was on Boyes Boulevard, I pulled my Jeep over to the side of the road and dialed Paul's home number. After a few rings, he answered.

"Are you with Henry?" he asked.

"No, I'm in Napa. Why would I be with Henry?"

"You were going to see him so I didn't know if you were there."

"No, I went yesterday." Paul's question threw me. "I'm still looking into it and I'll give you a full update when I have it, but I wanted to let you know that I'm close, Paul. I think I'm just one detail away. Which Roberto's getting for me."

"Are you with him right now?"

"No, I'm on my way to Alicia's house."

"Martin and Alicia? Do you think they're involved?" His voice was shaky.

"I don't know who's involved at this point. But in case I needed to talk to Alicia, I brought an empty bottle of an older Burgundy with me. Apparently she likes old wine labels. I just saw her at lunch and she said she'd like to see this one."

"Oh yes," replied Paul as relief flooded though his voice. "Katie, I think it's imperative that you only tell people that you're helping me with my cellar. I don't want anyone to know about the bottle yet."

"Of course. I'll give you a detailed update soon."

I put down the phone and continued driving until I reached Alicia and Martin's two-story house. It was Spanish style with white stucco and a red tile roof.

Bottle in hand, I climbed the steps to the front door and rang the bell. I waited next to a clay bowl planter with succulents on the patio.

No one answered.

The neighbor next door, an older lady with curly gray hair, eyed me suspiciously as she stood watering her lawn for much longer than necessary.

I politely smiled and rang the bell again. There was no answer.

Even though Alicia was expecting me, she might not be home from her errands yet. Or perhaps the bell was broken.

I lifted the iron owl-shaped knocker on the door and tapped it a few times, letting it land with a thud. The door opened an inch. "Hello," I called out. "Alicia? Martin?"

Hesitation filled me but curiosity won and I pushed the door open. The air inside was quiet and still.

"Martin? Alicia? Are you there?"

No response. Although I didn't want to go into the house uninvited, it wasn't the first time I had entered a house without permission. And Alicia knew I was coming. But I started to wonder if something was wrong. The door was open and Alicia had alluded to the fact that she would be home.

I stepped inside the hallway. The living room was decorated in a cheery style full of yellows and baby blues with flower-patterned couches and curtains.

"Alicia?" I called out as I walked along the hallway. My dad had investigated a few cases where family members or friends had been mistaken for intruders as they entered the residence. I wanted to make sure neither she nor Martin thought I was an intruder and accidentally shot me.

I stopped.

I *was* an intruder.

I turned to exit, the door to outside still open a few feet behind me. I could leave right now and get in touch with Alicia later to give her the bottle.

Or I could stay a few minutes longer and make sure she was okay. I turned and continued into the kitchen. White tile with blue curtains, and every tile along the counter was glazed with a wine label. Farther along the counter were a few wine bottles, same as any wine drinker, but I noticed most of the wine bottles were empty. I dismissed it, since I knew several people who liked to keep the empty bottles but then I noticed a funnel in the sink. It was a kitchen, but a funnel next to empty bottles of wine? My mind started to turn.

One bottle had a cork in it and I picked up the bottle. It was full, yet the cork had been removed and placed back in only halfway. Why would someone open a bottle of wine and then not drink any? And it was near a funnel. I held it up to look for the sediment.

"What are you doing here?"

I jumped and turned, the bottle slipping out of my grasp and breaking as it hit the floor, the wine filling the grooves between the tiles and spreading in every direction. Alicia stood in the doorframe, a shopping bag in each hand.

"I was looking for you," I stammered.

"How did you get in?"

"The door was open."

She put the bags on the center island. "You just walk into people's houses?"

"No, I ..." I faltered as I figured out how to get through this. "When I knocked on the door, I thought I heard you say to come in." Even as I said the lie, I knew it was incredibly unbelievable.

"That sounds unlikely," said Alicia. Clearly I wasn't the only one who didn't buy my fib. "Why are you here?"

I picked my bottle off the counter. "At lunch today, you said you might be interested in this label."

"No, I meant in my kitchen. I can remember a conversation from an hour ago. Normally visitors wait outside."

"Yes—" My sentence was cut off by Alicia's ear piercing scream.

She scrambled to the other side of the island. "What did you do to him? What did you do?"

"What?" I stepped over to the other side, where Martin lay on the floor. "No ..." I stared at Martin, his face pale and his eyes closed. "No," I repeated. "I only just got here."

"Martin! Martin!" Alicia patted his cheek. "Speak to me, sweetheart."

His eyes fluttered.

"I'm going to get you help. You'll be okay. You'll be okay." She stood up and grabbed her phone from the counter as she pointed her other hand at me. "Don't you move. Don't you move a single step."

SEVENTEEN

PAIRING SUGGESTION: MALBEC/CABERNET SAUVIGNON BLEND

—MENDOZA, ARGENTINA

A strong red wine that holds up over time.

༄

THE SONOMA SHERIFF STATION was buzzing with activity when I was brought in, but the room where I waited was eerily quiet. Perhaps they were built so that no one else could hear, or maybe I was the only one being questioned at that moment. Lucky me.

The door opened and two deputies, Adams and Garcia, entered. They were the same ones who had come to Paul's house, yet their demeanor was different today. Their looks of concern over Cooper's death were replaced by what should have been blank game faces but I could sense a hint of anger in their eyes.

"Katie Stillwell," said Adams as he sat down across the table. I took a deep breath as my lungs began to tighten. I wondered if Adams was going to play the good cop or the bad cop. Since they were in a team of two, I assumed one would take each role.

"Deputy Adams," I replied. "Deputy Garcia. Nice to see you again."

"I wish it were under different circumstances." Adams opened a file folder. "Why were you at the Trager residence?"

"Alicia was interested in wine labels. I was bringing her a bottle." I glanced around the empty room. "I had it with me…"

"Let's cut to the chase, shall we?" Adams said as he stared at me.

I waited, my game face on.

"What was your motivation for attacking Martin Trager?"

"I didn't."

Adams raised one eyebrow. "We should believe you, why?"

I waved a hand around to dismiss the anxiety building inside me. "I had just arrived. Someone must have attacked him before I was there."

"Mrs. Trager said she found you in her kitchen, standing over her husband," said Garcia.

"That's not true."

"So you weren't in her kitchen?"

I was digging myself into a hole. I needed to stick to the facts. But mostly I needed to be very precise. "I mean, I was in her kitchen but I wasn't standing over Martin. I didn't even know he was there until she came in and screamed."

"But you entered without permission."

I could fight this, but I knew he was right. And it wasn't the first time I had entered a house without permission. I had nearly been arrested for the same thing as a teenager, but Tessa covered for me.

"The front door was open. I was worried that there was something wrong. And I was right." It wasn't exactly the whole truth, but it would work. Or at least, it could work.

"Were you following Mrs. Trager?"

"If she arrived at the house after me, how could I be following her?" I leaned forward. "Listen, I was meeting her to give her the bottle. Ask her. She knew I was coming. In fact there was a witness to the invitation. Leanor Langley."

"Rosanna Davis," the deputy continued. "Does that name mean anything to you?"

I shook my head. A small tingle of panic began to creep up my arm. What was he talking about?

"She's a neighbor of Alicia and Martin. She said she didn't see anyone else go into their house, besides you."

I swallowed hard. It might be time to call a lawyer.

Adams flipped to the next page in his notebook. "Which leads me to my next question. Destroying Mrs. Trager's property."

"What property?" I thought back to the kitchen. "Do you mean the bottle of wine? That was an accident. I was looking at it and dropped it as she came in."

Adams leaned across the table. His aftershave was musky and pungent. "I think you were trying to steal it and dropped the evidence when she entered."

I stared at Adams. His five o'clock shadow seemed to get darker by the minute. Unlike with Dean and my father, I wasn't sure if being strong and looking him in the eye was going to get through to him, but I needed to be straightforward, declare my innocence, and tell him the truth.

"Deputy Adams, I was looking at the bottle in case it was fake. A counterfeit."

"What do you mean?"

"In case the wine inside was not what was on the label."

"Why would that matter to you? It's in Mrs. Trager's house, it's her business."

"It doesn't. I mean, it does." My anxiety was muddling my words. I took a breath, my lungs failing to reach their full capacity. I was going to have to proceed no matter what my anxiety was going to do. "I'm helping Paul Rafferty look into a counterfeit bottle of wine that he opened on Sunday. Paul told me not to tell anyone. Originally I thought Alicia could help me." My mind drifted to Roberto and his research and the phone call that would hopefully come any minute.

"Ms. Stillwell?"

"Sorry." I focused again. "She likes old wine labels, so I was taking her the bottle in case she had information. I saw her at lunch and she said to meet her at the house."

Adams nodded. "Paul Rafferty, huh?"

"Yes."

"Okay then." Garcia pulled out a second file from the stack and flipped it open on the table. "Since you mentioned Paul, let's talk about his assistant."

"Cooper? What about him?" I stared at Garcia. "You guys were there on Sunday. He fell down the stairs."

"Did he?" replied Adams.

"What? Now that you think I attacked Martin, you somehow believe I'm involved in Cooper's accident?" I shook my head. This wasn't going anywhere. "Look, this is all a big misunderstanding. I wanted to show Alicia the bottle. I went into the kitchen, she came in, saw Martin, and that was it. End of story."

"You're very verbose, aren't you?" said Adams.

I shifted in my seat but stayed silent. I didn't want him to think he was right.

"I was only going to ask how well you knew Cooper." Garcia moved the pages in the file.

I waited, unsure of how to answer. I didn't like where this was going. "Not too well. I mean, he came into my work, but I didn't know him outside of there."

The door opened. "Adams, we have an update."

"Excuse me for a moment." Adams stood up and left the room. Garcia stayed seated but silently flipped through the file.

I stared at the table as I thought about what I had seen at Alicia's. The door had been open, but nothing else seemed to be disturbed. No chairs tipped over, no signs of a struggle.

Adams returned to the room. "You're in luck. Martin is going to make it. Just a bad bump on the head, that's all."

"Good."

"Is it?" asked Adams.

"Yes, Martin was really nice when I met him at Paul's. I'm glad he's going to be okay. Not that you'll ever believe me."

"We believe you," said Adams.

"What?"

He nodded. "Martin said that someone hit him over the head but he doesn't think it was you."

"Someone asked him directly if it was me?"

"No. But in the statement at the hospital, he said his assailant was male. Mrs. Trager has also agreed not to press charges on breaking and entering."

"That's a relief." I pushed back the chair and stood up.

"We're not done here yet, Ms. Stillwell." Adams waited to continue speaking until I sat back down. "We're still talking about Cooper. You were the one who found him, correct?"

"Yes, but you knew that. I told you on Sunday." I stared at them. "Why all of these questions about Cooper?"

The deputies glanced at each other but didn't comment.

Garcia leaned back. "Is it true you were sitting next to him at dinner?"

"It was a small table. Most of us were sitting next to him." I sat straighter in my chair. "Is there something else going on?"

"Who served the wine that night?" asked Garcia.

"I did. Do you think I did something to him?"

Adams stared at me. "Is it just a coincidence you're working for Paul Rafferty now? Cooper's job."

I shook my head. "You really don't know me at all."

"I don't know you? I know you were involved in the murder at Frontier a few months ago."

"Rick," said Garcia, "leave her alone. You know she wasn't a part of that."

"Actually," I said as I put my arms on the table and smiled, "I was. I helped solve it."

"But now you have a new job."

"My job is still at Trentino, the same place where I've worked the last four years, and I love it. In the meantime, I'm working for Paul on a project about the counterfeit wine. Not as his assistant."

"Maybe this was your plan all along, to help Cooper down the stairs and then take his place." Adams stared at me.

"The agreement between me and Paul Rafferty has nothing to do with Cooper's accident. Besides, I was having dessert with the other guests when Cooper fell. There are witnesses." *If someone actually did help him down the stairs,* I thought to myself, *it wasn't me.*

The deputies glanced at each other. Adams closed the file and stared at me.

"Does this mean I can go? I'd like to get to work before my shift begins."

"You can leave, Ms. Stillwell," said Deputy Adams. "But know that I'm watching your every move."

EIGHTEEN

PAIRING SUGGESTION: CARIÑENA—ARAGON, SPAIN
*Cariñena or Carignan, primarily used as a blending grape
but has now become its own wine.*

༈

BY THE TIME I arrived at Trentino, I was nearly an hour late to my shift. I pulled open the door to the restaurant and paused when I saw Kurt by one of the tables, ready to work. That was fast. He asked Bill on Monday and a day later he already had a shift? I nodded at him as I walked by.

It's a funny thing about relationships. You can end them and step away, but sometimes life has a way of bringing you back together. Our relationship had come full circle. We had both worked at Trentino years ago, but it was only temporary before he moved to his position at Greco's. And here we were, working together again.

The evening went on as normal and I focused on the tables in my area until Kurt and I passed each other and our eyes met.

Even though I knew I still had feelings for him deep inside, there was no chance at reigniting the flame. It was history, and it needed to stay that way. Besides, I had Dean. Sort of. And I could never go back to Kurt. Not that things were bad, but I had a feeling from the moment we first met that it wasn't quite right with us. There wasn't an exact reason that I could put my finger on. It was similar to the moment in blind tasting when you had to make a call and you knew it wasn't going to be correct but you had no idea where else to turn.

I stood against the wall after the rush of tables had settled down. Kurt joined me a few minutes later. "Just like old times, working side by side."

"Yep." I focused on the tables, waiting to see if anyone needed anything. "But that was only briefly."

"You like to remind me of that."

"Sorry, I didn't mean it to sound that way."

Kurt turned to me. "You okay? You seem stressed."

He had always been able to read me. "I was questioned today at the sheriff's station. They thought I attacked someone."

"Did you?"

I looked at him. "Do you honestly think that I would?"

"No," he replied. "But I also don't know the situation, so I figured it was worth asking."

"No," I exhaled. "I didn't attack them. But being interrogated wasn't exactly how I wanted to spend my afternoon."

I watched the hostess, Alexis, motion to me as she sat a guest. I could tell by her signal that they had asked for me by name.

I approached the table to see Henry Diven. Although I wasn't exactly surprised—he had said he might stop by—it was still strange to see him sitting there.

"Welcome, Mr. Diven," I said as I stood at his table. "Have you dined with us before?"

"I haven't, actually. What would you recommend? I'd love a drink to get me started."

I thought back to the dinner at Paul's. "Perhaps a Manhattan?"

"No, I want a wine as an aperitif. Give me some of that sommelier knowledge."

"Champagne is an ideal aperitif. Shall I bring you a glass?"

"That sounds lovely," said Henry as he handed me the wine menu. "Make it the most expensive Champagne you have by the glass." He paused. "And actually, I'll probably have a steak for dinner so after the Champagne, a glass of Bordeaux. Your choice." He winked and the gesture didn't sit well with me. I didn't like people winking when they thought they knew me or, as I suspected in this case, thought they could control me. But I was glad he let me choose which wine to serve. This was a huge compliment coming from a wine enthusiast like him. Perhaps I was judging the wink too quickly. And then again, maybe I wasn't. I needed to keep my guard up.

When I finished delivering Henry's drinks, I returned to the wall. Kurt touched my arm. "I'm really sorry about your day."

I looked into his brown eyes. "You are?"

"Yes. Katie, even though you and I weren't good at dating, I still care for you as a friend. I always will."

"Thank you," I replied and smiled.

Two more tables were seated and I helped them with pairing suggestions and took their drink orders. One requested a Rioja Crianza, a Spanish wine made from the Tempranillo grape. I removed the foil from the bottle, cutting a perfect circle around the top, and inserted the opener into the cork. Every step I took was a moment of routine, method, and calmness. It helped shake off the day.

At the end of the night, Henry was my last table to leave. He sat with the paid check next to him and stared at me.

"Looks like you have a fan," said Kurt.

"Yep." I finally approached the table. "Mr. Diven, can I get you anything else?"

"No, I'm fine. It was a lovely evening."

"I'm glad to hear it. I hope you dine with us again."

He raised his eyebrows. "Do you?"

Game face on. "We love having repeat clientele," I said in a flat tone. In no way did I want him to think I was encouraging a relationship.

"Did you speak with Roberto?"

I glanced around. The nearby tables were empty. "I did. Thank you for the tip."

"Did he tell you more about the Chateau Clair Bleu?"

My instinct was to not trust Henry. Not to trust anyone, really. Especially now that people were being attacked. "We talked about the wine, yes. Thank you again for pointing me in his direction." I motioned to the bill. "Do you need anything else?"

"What did Roberto say?"

My mind raced to figure out how I should handle this. "I'm still sorting through what he told me."

"What was it?"

"I'm going to keep that information to myself for the time being."

Henry studied me. "I might be able to help, you know. I know people."

"Thank you," I replied. "I'll keep that in mind."

"Good," he said as he stood up. "Well, it was good seeing you. I hope to see you again soon. May I call you?"

"I think we should just leave it like this for now." I smiled and Henry got the hint, or at least I hoped he did.

He left and I waited inside the door of Trentino until I was certain that he had driven away.

Kurt pushed open the door. "Are you hanging around?"

"No, I'm leaving." I walked out of the restaurant and glanced around. I didn't see Henry waiting in his car. The coast was clear.

"Hey, it was fun working with you again. Looking forward to the next time," said Kurt.

"I agree." My phone started to ring. "Sorry, I've got to get that."

"No worries. See you tomorrow." Kurt headed to his car as I grabbed my phone without looking at the number.

"Hello?"

"Katie, it's Paul."

"Paul," I said with relief. "I've been meaning to call you. I just got off work."

"You may not have called, but Martin did."

"Martin?"

"Yes, he told me about what happened to him today."

"Is he feeling okay? I think they said it was a minor bump, right?" I nodded even though I was on the phone.

"He's fine. Resting at home now." Paul took a deep breath. "Katie, I think it's a good idea if we stop our project. I don't want you looking into the wine anymore."

"Why?"

He didn't answer.

"Paul, if you think that I had anything to do with Martin's attack—"

"Katie," he interrupted, "I can't have you working for me. It's not safe."

I glanced around the nearly empty parking lot and decided I should get into my car and lock the door. "Paul, I'll be fine. I know how to take care of myself."

There was a long silence. "No, that's not it."

A small ball of anxiety formed in my stomach.

"Katie, I shouldn't have hired you."

"What are you trying to say?"

"Martin is one of my closest friends and he was assaulted."

"I know, but Martin already said it wasn't me. Ask him yourself."

"I did. The truth is, he doesn't know who attacked him but he didn't want anyone associated with me to be charged. I need to be careful. I need to protect my reputation. Thank you for your help, but it stops here." He took another breath followed by a hoarse cough. "I'll pay you for the time you've already put into this. I'll have the check sent to Trentino."

"But Paul, you know you can trust me."

"I don't know who I can trust anymore." The phone call ended.

NINETEEN

PAIRING SUGGESTION: GAVI—PIEDMONT, ITALY

A white wine that is well balanced in both fruit and acidity.

◈

I OPENED THE DOOR to my apartment but stopped before stepping inside. There's a certain feeling that comes over you when you blind taste a wine you've had before—a familiarity that strikes you deep inside. It's the same feeling when you know something is awry before you can place it. That's what I felt as I stood at the door. I couldn't put my finger on it, but something was off. As if someone had been in there and looked around, careful not to touch anything but still leaving traces.

The flowers on the counter had lost the petals from one side, as if a shoulder had brushed against their fragile blooms. The couch cushions were shifted slightly from this morning, and my half-empty water glass on the table was closer to the edge.

But my laptop was still in the middle of the coffee table where I had left it the night before. Surely if someone was going to steal something, it would be my laptop.

I took one step inside, scanning for any additional details that I could peg down. My bed, a single with a blue cover, was exactly how I had left it—unmade. The books on my nightstand were in the same place as I remembered.

I began to doubt my suspicions. Maybe I had been wrong. After all, my computer was there. I sat down on the couch and glanced around one more time. I scanned the bookcase and that's when I saw it. A gap that wasn't there before, right between the end of the shelf and *The Wine Bible.* At first I couldn't place the item that was missing. I tried to tell myself that maybe I had pulled out a book and left it somewhere else, but as I stared at the space, I knew from the location that it was one I used frequently. Although I wasn't the tidiest person, I always put my books back.

And then I knew.

It was the black binder that contained all of my flash cards for the Certified and now the Advanced Exam. Thousands of them. Painstakingly handwritten over the last two years and placed into plastic sleeves where I could easily access them. Grouped into geographic regions with dividers, the cards were extensive and necessary for the test. And now they were gone.

Had I left the binder somewhere? My mind raced to the last time I had used it. Sunday night. I'd flipped through the pages after the dinner at Paul's and put it back in the bookcase when I was done.

Who would want my cards? Someone studying for the test? It didn't make sense. It was a pointed theft, something to unnerve me for whatever reason.

Robbed and fired on the same day. I didn't know which one was worse, but to steal my cards was just plain malicious.

I picked up my phone but paused. I didn't want to call the police. I had spent enough of my day being questioned. Even though I didn't live anywhere near Sonoma and the cops would definitely not be Adams and Garcia, I knew that they would find out about it. And even if the attending officers believed me, I doubted Adams would. He would never be convinced that someone broke into my apartment. Instead he would think that I had set this up as a diversion from the Martin and Cooper situations.

No, I needed someone else to help me. Someone to check things out.

I glanced up at the note on the bulletin board with Dean's phone number on it.

He arrived within an hour.

"Thanks for coming," I said as I opened the door to him. "Sorry for calling so late."

Dean nodded. "I didn't think I'd see you so soon after our lunch."

"Me either." I sighed. "The rest of my day has not been so great."

"Cute place." Dean glanced around my four-hundred-square-foot apartment. "You live alone?"

I was a little embarrassed that I hadn't made the bed, but I wasn't used to visitors, especially unexpected ones. "I prefer it that way. No one to fight with over the dinner leftovers."

"You're that into leftovers?"

"Listen, I love Thai food. And when I'm craving those leftovers, I like coming home knowing they're still there."

Dean smiled and then became serious. "Okay, so you say someone broke in?"

"Yes."

His gaze drifted to my computer on the table. "What was taken?"

I pointed to the bookshelf. "My flash card binder. For my exam."

Dean took out his notebook and wrote it down. "What else?"

"That's it."

He stared at me, his blue eyes emotionless. "Did you check everywhere?"

"Yes. That's all that was taken."

He lowered his notebook. "You're telling me someone broke into your apartment just to steal your flash cards?"

I shrugged. "Yep."

"Are you sure you didn't leave them somewhere? I mean, I know you said they were stolen, but maybe you went to a study group and left them there."

"No, I looked at them Sunday night. I know they were here."

Dean looked at me. "You should really call the San Francisco Police."

"No more police."

"What do you mean?"

I filled him in on my day.

"Katie, I'm worried about you. Martin was attacked moments before you were there, and now your apartment has been broken into. You need to report this."

"No." I shook my head. I didn't want to go down that road. "It's not a valuable theft. At least not to anyone else."

"But it is to you," he added.

I nodded. "Those cards took me countless hours and over two years of research."

"This doesn't appear to be the work of a career criminal. Your laptop would be gone, for one thing."

"No. This was personal."

Dean paced around the living room and took a moment to inspect the door lock. "It doesn't look like it was jimmied open. Who has a key?"

"Besides me, no one. I mean, the building's super, but that would be it and I highly doubt he would have stolen my flash cards."

Dean shook his head. "If it wasn't with a key then they had to get in another way. I don't like the idea of you here by yourself when someone can get in. You should get your lock changed." He glanced around. "Just the two windows?"

"There's also a small one in the bathroom."

Dean disappeared into the bathroom and returned to the main room, checking both windows. "Katie, come here. This one's open."

"What?"

"Take a look."

I stepped closer to the large window that faced the side alley. The brass hook, which kept the sides together, was undone.

"I must have opened it one day and forgotten." I glanced outside. "I guess I never thought about someone coming up the fire escape."

Dean latched the window. "I still want you to be safe, so do me a favor and get the door lock changed. Even if you think the super is the only one with a key. It's better to be safe." He paused. "In fact, I'll pick up a lock and do it myself tomorrow. Is that okay?"

I smiled. "That would be great. Thanks." I rubbed my arms.

"You okay?"

"Yeah. Just unsettled." I sank down onto the edge of the sofa.

Dean took a seat next to me. "Any thoughts on who could have done this?"

"Not sure. Someone who knew I was studying for the next exam."

"Isn't that everyone?"

"Pretty much." I glanced at Dean, his blond hair falling to the side of his face. "Do you think this is related to Martin's attack?"

He sighed. "It's strange that they both happened on the same day. But I don't understand the flash card thing. Could this be someone from your tasting group?"

"No, we're good friends. I trust them completely." Kurt went through my mind. But he wouldn't do that. He was perhaps a little bitter, but not mean. And we had just worked together and everything was fine.

"Does everyone in your group know where you live?"

"Of course." I paused as it dawned on me. "But if this is somehow related to Paul, there is someone from the dinner who knows where I live. He dropped me off yesterday." I glanced at the clock. It was nearly two in the morning on Wednesday. "I mean two days ago. Simon Watkins. He gave me a ride on Monday."

"Maybe he broke in."

I shrugged. "I have no idea what he would do with flash cards. Or why he would take them from me."

"Maybe because you're working for Paul."

"Well, not anymore. Paul fired me earlier tonight."

"Why?"

"He was worried I might have attacked Martin. I mean, I *was* there when it happened. Or right after. But he wasn't sure, so he fired me."

"Sorry to hear that." Dean studied me for a while. "Do you think the same person who attacked Martin could have done this? Like a warning, to tell you to stop?"

"No," I replied, but Dean didn't look like he believed me. And to be honest, neither did I.

TWENTY

PAIRING SUGGESTION: TOURIGA NACIONAL

—ALTO DOURO, PORTUGAL

A full-bodied red wine made from a thick-skinned grape.

❧

AFTER A FEW HOURS of sleep and a hot shower, the Wednesday meeting with my blind tasting group was a welcome dose of normalcy. I was no longer working with Paul and my flash cards were gone, but there were still five glasses of wine that needed to be identified.

After the tasting group, I stood outside the private dining room and stared across the restaurant. Part of me wondered if Paul would come in for lunch again, but he wasn't in his favorite booth.

"You okay?" Bill studied me as he stood at my side.

"Yeah," I lied. "Just taking a moment."

"Sure," he said. "But I've known you for four years. Something else is going on."

I took a deep breath. "Paul Rafferty fired me last night and then someone broke into my apartment."

Darius exited the dining room and joined us. "Someone robbed you? You okay?"

"Yeah, I'm fine. I wasn't home."

"How much did they take?"

A nervous laugh escaped from my lips. "Well, it wasn't how much they took, it was what they took. Only one thing. My flash cards." It sounded ridiculous, even to me.

"Your flash cards?" Darius folded his arms as Kurt joined the three of us, his bag on his shoulder.

"Yep. My entire binder."

"That's so pointed." Bill understood. He knew the hours and tediousness of preparing the cards.

"I know. All of that time and energy spent making those and now they're probably at the bottom of a trashcan."

"I wouldn't say that. Maybe someone else is studying them," Bill added.

"I doubt it. I can't imagine anyone else would actually use them."

"Sorry about the cards," said Kurt. "You know, if you did them on your phone, you wouldn't have to worry about them being stolen. There'd be a backup."

"I like using the real ones. Besides, I feel I learn from writing things down." I sighed. "Except now they're gone. All of them." I shrugged. "It's a temporary setback. When I'm ready, I'll start over and make them again, one by one."

"Cause if you want something badly enough—"

"You make it happen." I finished Bill's sentence. "Besides, if they're trying to distract me from studying, they've failed. It's only going to make me more focused." I breathed out. "See you in a few hours." I was on the schedule for later in the day, but I wanted to go home and change and maybe pick up the pack of colored flash cards Cooper had given me. Maybe it was time to start from the beginning.

I walked out of Trentino and saw a figure standing near my car. It was too far away for me to recognize but knowing that Martin had been attacked and someone knew where I lived, my guard was up. I continued to approach, knowing that I could grab my wine opener from my purse if needed. Although it was small, it did have a knife on it.

I realized it was Dean.

"Hey." Relief flowed through me as I approached him. "I'm glad it's you."

"Hey," he replied with a smile on his face.

"Don't you ever work?" I winked.

"I'm a detective, I go where I'm called. And you did call me last night." He held up a key and handed it to me. "All done."

"Is that for my new lock?"

"Yep. Drove back this morning and took care of it."

"Thanks. I really appreciate it."

"It was my pleasure. I want to make sure my friends are safe."

My focus from Dean was distracted as a car pulled into the lot. A black Mercedes Sedan. Simon's car.

"Oh, it's him."

"What?"

"That's Simon. He's the one that gave me the ride."

Dean stared at the car. "Do you think he's the one who broke in?"

"Who knows?"

Simon hopped out at valet and handed over his keys. He noticed me and walked over.

"Katie." He looked at Dean and then back at me. "I'm so sorry about everything with Paul. It's really terrible and unfair."

Dean and I glanced at each other. Clearly Simon had heard that Paul had fired me. "I'll be fine."

Simon raised his eyebrows. "Wait, why will you be fine?"

I paused as I took in the situation. "Isn't that what you were saying was so terrible, that he fired me?"

"He fired you? Why?"

"It doesn't matter." I paused as I decided how to broach the subject. I chose blunt and to the point. "Simon, someone broke into my apartment last night."

Simon's face fell. "I'm very sorry to hear that."

I glanced at Dean and then back at Simon. "You know where I live. You gave me a ride home."

Simon stared at me. "What are you implying?"

"Did you go to my apartment?"

"Are you serious?"

"Yes."

"Katie, why would I do that? What would be the reason?"

"I don't know. That's why I'm asking."

"Are you sure you didn't stop by?" added Dean.

I shot him a look, hoping to convey that I was fine handling this on my own.

Simon shook his head. "Katie, it could have been anybody but it definitely was not me. It's not hard to find out where someone lives these days." He motioned with his hand. "Why would you even think it was someone you know? Burglaries happen all the time."

"Because I was working for Paul. Looking into a wine." I stopped speaking. I didn't want to share more information unless I had to. "That doesn't matter, but it's clear it was someone I know because of what they took."

Simon straightened his jacket. "Listen, Katie. I don't know what your situation was with Paul but if you think someone is after you, you need to be careful. There may come a point, which you might have already reached, where I won't be able to help you."

"Why would you be able to help her?" asked Dean.

"I'm saying I won't be able to," replied Simon as he focused solely on me and not Dean. "It's complicated. But if someone broke in, you might already be outside of my realm." He smiled but his eyes had a strong level of concern in them. "Just be careful." Simon glanced over his shoulder at the restaurant's entrance.

"Why are you here at Trentino? Was this just to warn me?"

"I'm meeting a friend for lunch." He looked at his watch. "Actually, I'm already late."

"I haven't seen you here before."

Simon motioned to my casual attire. "I guess you don't work lunch." He tilted his head. "Am I not allowed to dine at your restaurant now that you think I robbed you? Listen, I don't know what was taken, but if officials are looking into it, have them check out my alibi. I was in Healdsburg for business all day yesterday. I have bigger things to worry about than petty theft." He closed the button of his suit. "If you'll excuse me, I have a luncheon to attend."

"Wait," I said as Simon stepped away. "You never said what was so terrible about Paul."

"Oh, didn't you hear? He was arrested for Cooper's murder this morning. He just posted bail about an hour ago."

TWENTY-ONE

PAIRING SUGGESTION: VALPOLICELLA SUPERIORE—VENETO, ITALY

A versatile wine with flavors of black cherry,
it's ideal for those who like big red wines.

❧

DEAN AND I STOOD silent as we watched Simon enter Trentino.

"I can't believe Cooper was murdered," I finally stated. "I mean, I had a suspicion, but I can't believe I was right." I shook my head. "But it wasn't Paul. He didn't even leave the room when Cooper did. He couldn't have pushed him."

"I'm sure he'll get a great legal team together."

"Maybe," I replied as my mind raced through how many times I had met Paul. He didn't come across as a murderer.

"Katie," said Dean. "I can tell you're deep in thought. What's going on?"

"Paul didn't kill Cooper. I'm sure of it. And it's not like he altered the stairs. I went down those same stairs just after Cooper and I was fine. The top one was a little loose but nothing to cause an accident."

"What are you getting at?"

"I think someone's trying to set Paul up. Just like somebody broke into my place last night and like someone attacked Martin. This has to do with Paul's wine."

"But Katie, if the deputies arrested him for murder, they must have had a good reason."

I looked at Dean. "You mean something bigger than Cooper just falling down the stairs?"

He nodded.

"No one said murder in reference to Cooper's death, but the deputies were pressing me with questions yesterday and it's starting to make a little more sense. There's a reason they think Paul murdered Cooper, and I need to find out what it is."

"How will you do that?"

I unlocked my car. "By calling Paul and seeing if I can help."

Dean stepped closer. "I don't want to act like the voice of reason here, but you don't work for him anymore. He fired you and he's been arrested for murder. Maybe you should be careful around him. Not that I want to put any trust in what that Simon guy said, but things might be getting dangerous."

"Look what happened with my apartment. They already know I'm involved. Besides, Paul's health hasn't been great recently. This could be devastating to him. If there really is a murder investigation going on, I can help."

"You shouldn't give help until you're asked for it. Isn't that how you view life?"

I stared into Dean's blue eyes. "Yes." I paused. "But if it turns out Cooper really was murdered, everyone at that dinner is a suspect." *Including me,* I wanted to add, but I kept that to myself. I took my phone out of the car. "The least I can do is check on him. See if he's okay. I promise I'll be careful."

Dean nodded and watched as I dialed.

It rang and I started to think Paul might not pick up. He was under investigation for murder. The last thing he needed was a phone call from someone he had just fired.

"Hello," he said in a weak voice.

"Paul, it's Katie Stillwell. I heard about the …" My voice fell away. I wasn't sure what to say. "The arrest. I'm so sorry, but I want you to know that I don't think you're involved. And I want to help."

There was a long pause.

"Can you come over right away?"

TWENTY-TWO

PAIRING SUGGESTION: PINOT BLANC—ALSACE, FRANCE
Subtle and discreet, this wine has soft honey flavors
with a small amount of acidity.

☙

THE DRIVE TO PAUL'S house in Sonoma felt completely different this time, the excitement of opening a rare and expensive bottle replaced by the possibility of a murder investigation.

I glanced at the vineyards as I drove, their branches bare as they waited for the bud break in the spring. Still, the order of their straight, organized lines gave me strength.

The house came into view, but it looked much different in the daylight, as if it carried an air of sadness.

I arrived at the gate and buzzed the intercom.

"Hello," said a weak voice, a strong contrast to Cooper's jovial greeting on Sunday.

"Paul, it's Katie."

My comment was met by silence on the intercom. I put the car in park and waited. Perhaps my long drive had been pointless after all.

Then the gate opened. I took a deep breath as I drove up the driveway and parked. I needed to be calm and collected. I needed to be strong.

I arrived at the front door just as Paul opened it. He looked pale and tired, his blue eyes void of energy. "Come in."

I stepped inside and followed him down the marble hallway.

We reached the sitting area and Paul leaned against the bar, his focus centered on the wall in front of him.

"How are you?" I stood next to Paul, not wanting to sit.

"Well, let's see," he said as his emotionless stare focused on me. "I paid a lot of money for a fake bottle of wine, my assistant is dead, and now I'm being blamed for his murder. Not exactly great."

"I'm so sorry." I swallowed hard. I knew there had to be more to the story and it was time to find out. There had to be a reason Paul was under suspicion.

"Paul, this morning..." My voice fell away. "Why did they arrest you? You were in the living room when he fell. I'm a witness. All of us here were witnesses."

He shook his head. "That's not the part that they're talking about. There's more."

I leaned forward. "Paul, Cooper didn't just fall, did he?"

Paul gripped my arm. "No."

I took a deep breath but it didn't satisfy me as my lungs refused to expand. I never liked to hear bad news. I preferred stories about wine. Not about death. "What happened? Did they tell you?"

Paul released his hold and reached for a bottle of whiskey. His hand shook as he poured two fingers into a glass and then took a long sip. "He was poisoned," he said.

My mind raced. Poisoned? I waited for Paul to speak as he focused his attention on me.

"At my dinner. With my friends. Murdered."

I looked into Paul's eyes, searching for more information, but he didn't give any. "I don't understand. I found him at the bottom of the stairs."

Paul shook his head. "Now they're saying he fell because of the poison. That he must have ingested it at dinner or shortly after."

"But we all ate the same food. Drank the same wine." I swallowed hard. Could it have been the Chateau Clair Bleu?

Paul took another sip as his hand continued to shake.

I wondered if the hand tremors were from the stress or a medical condition. I motioned to the barstool and helped him sit.

"Exactly," said Paul. "We all drank and ate the same thing. He must have had it separately."

"Which means he was targeted," I replied without meaning to say it out loud. "But why do they think you poisoned him? Why were you arrested out of everyone here that night?"

Paul put down the empty glass. "I have no idea. It was my party, perhaps. Cooper worked for me. I don't know."

I moved the bottle closer to him.

"I'm not sure what's worse," he said as he poured another shot of whiskey. "Being arrested for a crime I didn't commit, or knowing that one of my friends is a murderer." He looked at me. "Katie, what am I supposed to do?"

He was in a tough situation and I didn't know how to respond, but I needed to think clearly. "Paul, why would anyone at the table that night kill Cooper? What would be the reason?"

"I have no idea. They were all my friends." He looked into my eyes. "But I can trust you."

"You fired me yesterday. You said you didn't trust me."

He shifted his gaze down at the bar. "I was in a different place then. That was because things were happening. Martin was attacked." Paul's voice turned into a whisper. "Today it's different. I need someone who couldn't have been involved with what happened to Cooper. And I believe in my heart that you had nothing to do with it. That's not who you are."

"No, it's not. Paul, did anyone that night have any grievances against Cooper?"

Paul shook his head. "No. None that I knew, anyway. Everyone at the dinner loved him. They'd all known him for years. It just seems so random. First a counterfeit wine and then a murder."

And that was when it dawned on me. I sank onto the nearby stool. "Paul, what if it's because of the wine? I told Cooper that it was a forgery and he was going to check on it. What if him checking meant talking to someone else at the dinner? And they were involved with the wine so they killed him?"

"Involved with the wine? But I bought it at the auction."

"What if they're connected?"

Paul stared off into the distance. "Prior to this morning, I would have said that's not possible, but now I don't know." He turned his attention to me. "Thanks for coming here. On the phone you said you could help. I know the deputies will be looking into it, but they think I'm guilty. And even if there are some officers who don't, they're busy with other cases. I need someone who's focused solely on this." He paused. "Besides, I know about you. I've heard things." He swirled his whiskey and took another drink as my adrenaline level skyrocketed.

What had he heard? About my past? That I had broken into a house years ago? That I had been arrested a few months back when someone planted evidence against me? The pressure was getting to me but I didn't want to show that to Paul. I took a deep breath and waited as he finished his whiskey.

Paul put his glass down and smiled. "The work you did at Frontier. It's no secret here in Sonoma. I know that you solved that whole thing. Your friend Tessa was blamed and instead you figured it out and put the right people in jail." He stared at me. "Where would she be without you? She didn't do it and I didn't do this. I'll pay you to help." Paul's voice was weak and it was followed by a raspy cough.

Stress like this could have devastating effects on people, and I didn't know if Paul's cough was the hint of something worse.

"Paul, you don't need to pay me."

"It's not up for debate." His pale blue eyes stared into mine. "So you'll help?"

"Consider me rehired."

"Thank you." He smiled weakly. "Where will you start? None of this makes sense."

I thought back to the dinner when Cooper disappeared from the sitting room to look for the second bottle. "Paul, you bought two bottles at the auction, correct? I think Cooper said they were from the same seller?"

"Yes," Paul replied. "A Chateau Valence."

The phone rang and he jumped.

"Can I see that bottle? It's what Cooper was going to look at Sunday night."

The phone continued to ring and Paul seemed frailer by the moment. "Do you want me to answer it?" I asked.

He looked at the phone. "It's fine. Is it strange that even though I'm out on bail, I think they're going to come back for me any moment? It was horrible being arrested. I've never been so embarrassed in my life."

"Don't worry, we're going to figure this out." I motioned to the still-ringing phone. "I'm sure it'll go to voicemail any second."

"I should answer it. It could be my lawyer. The bottle's in the cellar. I'll meet you there in a minute." He handed me the key.

I returned to the hallway, an uneasy feeling washing over me as I remembered the last time I was there. When I found Cooper.

I unlocked the cellar door and turned on the light, the one I couldn't find that night because the switch was located outside the doorway. I went down the stairs but paused on the last step as I stared at the floor. My stomach soured as the memory of finding him played out in my mind.

I took a deep breath and moved over the area with one large jump, as if touching the ground there would be disrespectful to Cooper.

The cellar was narrow with two rows of bottles stacked in perfectly symmetrical cedar racks. I scanned the lines for the bottle of Chateau Valence, my heart accelerating as I saw bottles of Mouton Rothschild, Chateau Margaux, d'Yquem, Domaine Garinett, and even a Chateau Lafite Rothschild. It was a wine lover's paradise.

"Did you find it?" Paul's voice made me jump.

I put my hand to my chest in an effort to calm my breathing. "I didn't hear you come down."

"Sorry about that," said Paul as he joined me in the row. "My lawyer's on the way as well as the deputies. Something about evidence. Did you find it? The 1989 Chateau Valence."

"Not yet." I scanned the rows. "Do you know where you put it?"

Paul pointed to a row. "It was right here."

I followed the line of his finger, but it ended at an empty space in the middle of the rack. "It's gone."

TWENTY-THREE

PAIRING SUGGESTION: CABERNET SAUVIGNON BLEND
—COLCHAGUA VALLEY, CHILE

A bold red wine ideal for storing, as it ages very well.

❧

I STARED AT THE empty space located between a Chateau Margaux and a St. Emillion. "Are you sure it was there?"

"Positive. I kept the 1975 Chateau Clair Bleu in the dining room and placed the Chateau Valence here, to save for a future occasion."

I scanned the rest of the racks to make sure the Chateau Valence hadn't been moved while Paul looked on the other side. He was right. The bottle was gone.

"When was the last time you saw it there?"

"I don't know." He rubbed his forehead. "I was down here on Sunday, moments before the guests arrived. Cooper had already brought bottles into the lounge, but I wanted a d'Yquem for dessert. He was greeting guests at the front door." Paul stopped. "Probably Leanor and Simon. Maybe Henry, too. So I came down to the cellar and found the bottle myself. The d'Yquem." He looked at me. "That's why I was late coming to greet you in the lounge after you arrived."

"Has anyone had access to the cellar? Who else is in the house?"

"Just Anna, but she wouldn't have been in here. I keep the door locked. I have the only key."

I glanced at the stairs. "But Cooper came down here that night. How did he get in? What about his key?"

"I had the door open. I didn't lock it after I left with the d'Yquem. I thought I might show them the cellar after dinner. They'd seen it on past visits, everyone except for you, but I've found that guests get a thrill at seeing my collection." He looked around. "Or at least I thought they did."

I rubbed my arms. The coolness of the cellar was starting to get to me. "And since then? Since Sunday?"

"It's been locked."

"Okay." I looked at the row of bottles, all waiting for their moment to be opened and enjoyed. Except for the one bottle that was missing. "Who would have taken it?"

Paul shrugged. "I don't know. There were my guests at dinner that night and then the deputies."

"I doubt the deputies would have taken it."

"Really? Couldn't it be evidence?"

"Yes," I replied. "But did you tell them about the bottle? That you bought it at the auction as well?" I realized as I spoke that I was coming across as if I were interrogating him. I softened my tone. "I mean, that night they thought it was an accident on the stairs. There was no reason for them to take any wine bottles. Did other people know that you bought it at the auction?"

Paul looked at me. "Everyone at the dinner did. It wasn't a secret that I purchased two bottles."

Great. The list of suspects wasn't getting any smaller. As with deductive tasting, I needed to start crossing potential wines—or in this case, people—off the list to narrow it down to the right one.

"We know that Cooper was poisoned and any member of the group could have accessed Cooper's wineglass or food at any time. But if it was the wine…" I paused. I liked to think of wine bringing happiness instead of death. "It could have easily been tampered with when we moved from the dining room to the sitting room for dessert. Besides you and me, there were six other guests here: Henry, Simon, Leanor, Alicia, Martin, and Roberto. Those are the suspects. Six. Actually, seven."

"Seven?"

"Anna."

Paul shook his head. "No, not Anna. I trust her. She's worked for me for years."

"But you trust everyone from the dinner as well, right?"

"As much as I can." Paul sighed. "In the years at my firm, I learned that most of my clients had something to hide. I trust them until I'm given a reason not to."

I walked the length of a row, staring at the bottles as my mind turned. "If this had something to do with the counterfeit bottle of wine, Anna wouldn't have a motive. I'm going to focus on the remaining six." It was still seven, but I didn't want to say it. Not that I believed Paul did it, but I couldn't leave him off the list. If I was going to solve this, I needed to explore every single possibility.

He leaned back, the overhead light casting a shadow on his face. "What are you going to do?"

"I guess I'm going to start narrowing down the field of suspects until we have the one responsible. I've already talked with Roberto, Henry, and Simon. I guess Leanor and Alicia would be next."

"You haven't named the one person I think you should talk to." The intercom buzzed. "That will be the deputies or my lawyer at the gate."

"Who should I talk to?"

"Martin."

"Martin?" My chest tightened. "Yes, but he told you he wasn't sure who attacked him. And that there was a chance it could be me. Which it wasn't."

"I know, but he's my best friend and I know he's looking out for me.

"Paul, I don't want to say this, but he was at the dinner that night. He could have been ..." I stopped speaking. I needed to say this gently. "Everyone is a suspect."

"Go talk to him. He knows everyone from the dinner better than me. He'll be able to help you."

"Will he even talk to me?"

"I'll call him and let him know you're coming."

Paul gave me Martin's work address and I was on my way.

The squad car pulled into the driveway as I left the estate. Deputy Adams stared at me as I drove by. It wasn't exactly a statement to my innocence, being back at the scene of the crime when Adams already seemed to suspect me. He would know why I was there sooner than later, perhaps in just a few minutes when he talked to Paul. For now, I was on my way to see Martin.

TWENTY-FOUR

PAIRING SUGGESTION: CÔTES DU RHÔNE—RHÔNE VALLEY, FRANCE

*A Grenache- or Syrah-based blend
that is popular and very drinkable.*

❧

MARTIN'S OFFICE WAS LOCATED a few blocks from downtown Sonoma in a two-story house that had been converted into an office
building. A neighboring vineyard stretched out behind it, adding a
sense of calm to the situation and loosening the tightness in my
chest.

I pulled the brass handle, bells jangling as the door opened to a
hallway. The noise must have announced my presence because as
soon as I put a foot inside, a young man in a dark vest and matching
pants with his blue sleeves rolled up to his elbows approached me.

"Welcome to Trager Imports. What can I help you with?"

"I'm here to see Martin Trager."

"Do you have an appointment?" He held one hand tucked into
the opening of his vest between buttons, in a clearly rehearsed man-
ner to project a certain appearance of power.

"No, but Mr. Paul Rafferty said he would call and let Martin know I was coming."

"Name?"

"Katie Stillwell."

"Just a moment." He turned on his heels and walked down the hallway.

As I waited, I could hear typing and a printer that sounded like it was seconds away from a paper jam.

The man returned, his hand still tucked into the vest. "He said he'll see you but he only has a few minutes."

"That will be fine."

He motioned to a doorway down the hall.

I entered the office and there was Martin, sitting at a desk with a large map on the wall behind him. He had a bandage over the left side of his forehead.

"Katie, it was a surprise when Paul called to say you were coming. I'm glad you're here." He stood up and reached out his hand.

The welcome gesture threw me. "You are?" I shook his hand, his grip folding the sides of my palm together.

"Yes. Come on, we both know that you didn't attack me." As he said it, he seemed to reference my strength.

I pulled my hand out of his grasp. I was stronger than he knew. I could attack him if I wanted to, I was sure of it. But I wouldn't do that to anyone.

"Because you didn't. Right, Katie?"

"Right," I replied. "But you said to Paul last night that you didn't know who assaulted you, you just didn't want me to be charged. You made him believe it might still be me."

Martin waved his hand. "My head was still foggy at that point and I honestly don't know who attacked me. But I know it wasn't you. Do you want me to call and tell Paul?"

"No, Paul and I are fine now. Do the officers have any idea who it was?"

Martin touched the bandage on his head. "Not yet. It could be an unhappy customer, a neighbor with a grievance, or simply a burglary gone wrong. These things always have a way of coming into the light." He sat in the chair behind his desk and motioned to the chair in front.

I sat down as my attention drifted to the map. It detailed an area with varying shades of green and a long river with tributaries marked in blue. "Where is that?"

"Willamette. I have some property up there."

"Beautiful area."

He leaned back and folded his hands on his stomach. "It is. So what can I help you with?"

I sat up straighter in my seat. "I want to know if you saw anything strange that night at the dinner. Anything out of the ordinary."

"Well, it's not every day that we're treated to a bottle of wine from 1975, now is it?"

I smiled, my game face on.

"That, and someone was murdered. Poor Cooper. To think that someone killed him. It's devastating."

"How do you know he was murdered?"

"Paul told me this morning, after he made bail. What a week." Martin picked up a pen from a silver holder and scribbled a note on a pad to his right.

"Do you think Paul did it?"

Martin raised an eyebrow. "Does the fact that you're asking mean *you* think Paul did it?"

"No, that's not what I'm saying." I took a breath. "I want to know what you think."

"An opinion can be a dangerous thing, Katie." He looked me in the eye. "But no, I don't think Paul killed Cooper. Why would a man as rich and powerful as Paul want to kill his assistant? When you have that much money, you can pay someone to kill them for you."

"I don't—"

"Listen," Martin interrupted, "I'll get to the point. Even if Paul had something to do with Cooper's death, he wouldn't have done it on an evening with his closest friends as witnesses. Agreed?"

I nodded. This wasn't going where I needed it to go.

"But I don't think Paul killed him. He wouldn't kill anyone. We've been friends a very long time and he's a good guy."

"Paul says you're one of the few people who don't think he's guilty."

Martin smiled. "You're right. I don't. He's a good man."

"What about anyone else?"

"You mean, did I see who poisoned him? No. If I had, I would have spoken up that night." Martin fell silent as he stared at the desk in front of him. "We were all friends there, but I've been thinking ... Maybe the person who poisoned Cooper is the same one who attacked me."

"I was wondering that, too," I replied. "But why would they want to kill Cooper and attack you? What would you have to do with this?"

Martin shrugged. "Maybe because I was at the dinner. I don't know. I wish I did." He studied me for a moment. "Are you working for Paul?"

I stiffened. "Why do you say that?"

"It seems like you're asking questions for him. You're not exactly one of his friends, and now that Cooper is gone ..." He paused. "It's just an observation. Doesn't Trentino pay well?"

I shifted in the chair as my mind raced to come up with an answer. "It's fine, but I could always use some more. Might be nice to attend one of those great charity dinners Alicia mentioned on Sunday," I replied in an effort to connect to him.

Martin nodded. "You know, we have some openings and could always use the help of someone as experienced in wine as you are. Would you like to work for us here?"

"Thanks, but I think I'm good at the moment."

"Working for Paul," Martin added, as if he wanted to confirm his guess. "Do you have any more questions or shall I get back to work?"

"One. I wanted to ask about the Red Heart auction. Paul bought two different wines there ..."

"Yes, the ones he bought from Simon."

Goosebumps shot up my arms. "Simon sold the bottles at the auction?"

"Didn't you know?"

I shook my head as I tried to realize the weight of this information. "I only knew it was a private party. But why would Simon sell the bottles?" And more importantly, why would he sell them and not tell anyone at the dinner?

"Why does anyone sell bottles of wine at auction?" commented Martin. "Money. Isn't that reason enough?"

I paused. "Did Paul know that Simon was the seller?"

"I doubt it. I only knew because I was at the auction with Henry."

"But Roberto had the bottle before Simon did."

"What's that?"

"Nothing," I replied. "Just talking to myself."

Martin touched his bandaged head and winced.

"Are you okay?"

"Katie," said Martin. "I'm so sorry, but my head is really starting to hurt. Do you mind if we talk about this later?"

"Of course. That's fine. But if you remember anything from that night…"

"You'll be the first one I call."

"Thank you." I stood up. "Feel better."

"I'll be fine. Stay well, Katie."

I walked out of the office knowing one thing. Simon was hiding something and like an unidentified glass of wine in blind tasting, I needed to figure it out.

TWENTY-FIVE

PAIRING SUGGESTION: BRUNELLO DI MONTALCINO

—MONTALCINO, ITALY

Made from 100% Sangiovese grapes,
this red wine pairs well with game.

☙

I CALLED PAUL FROM my car as I left Trager Imports. "Paul, I just talked to Martin. He said Simon was the private party who sold the bottle at the auction."

"Simon? But why didn't he say something?"

"I don't know. I know he bought it from Grand Vino, but something doesn't match up. I'm still waiting on the name from Roberto, of where it was before then, but there's more here. I'm heading to work now but I'll keep investigating tomorrow."

"Thank you, Katie. I appreciate it." He coughed.

I started driving but I wanted to grab food before I got too far. I needed to eat on my way, since I wouldn't have a chance otherwise before my shift.

I pulled into the Waterson Market and bought a caprese sandwich, as I loved mozzarella, tomatoes, and basil.

I returned to my car but noticed a black Mercedes Sedan parked across the lot. The same kind Simon drove. I sat in my driver's seat and decided to eat my sandwich while I waited to see who would approach the Mercedes. I needed to leave for work soon, but curiosity was getting the best of me.

And there he was, Simon.

I got out of the car and approached him. He was loading groceries into the trunk when I reached him. "Simon?"

He turned around, looking surprised. "Katie, what are you doing here?"

"Listen, I have to talk to you."

He glanced around.

"I found out that you were the one who sold the Chateau Clair Bleu at the auction. Why didn't you tell me before?"

"Why would I tell you?" He shook his head. "I don't understand."

"I mean, why wouldn't you mention it at the dinner?"

Simon shrugged. "Why would it matter?"

I stared at him. It was time to put the cards on the table. "Because it was counterfeit."

The color drained from Simon's face. "You know?"

"Yes," I replied. "Paul and I both know."

Simon glanced around the parking lot as he closed the trunk. "It's not safe for you to be seen with me right now. I don't know who's watching."

A chill crept up my spine, but I was also suspicious. Simon was dodging the question.

He unlocked the driver's door and sat down. "Listen, this thing is way out of hand and if you know the bottle is fake, then I'm in a lot of danger and so are you." He looked around again. "Is this what your project with Paul is about?"

I nodded.

"I knew I shouldn't have sold that bottle. I've been in over my head for a while but I think things are about to go south in a big way." He put his hand to his chin. "Okay, here's what needs to happen. The only way to get around it is to take them down but I need help. I need you and Paul." He looked around again. "I can't talk here. Follow me to my house, but not too close behind. When you get to my house, wait a few minutes before coming inside. I don't want people to see us together."

"I don't have time, Simon. You need to tell me now."

"I can't. If I don't give you evidence, the extra counterfeit bottles, no one will believe you. And then it will be too late." Simon started the car. "Go, now." His voice had an edge of fear to it.

I returned to my car. I knew I should leave the rest of the investigating to the sheriff's deputies. Martin had been attacked and my apartment had been burglarized. But if I was in more danger, I needed to find the best way out of it. I hesitated but my curiosity got the best of me. I decided I would follow Simon and stay for a few minutes but keep my guard up while I was there.

I kept several car lengths between us, following him at a slow pace. We entered Glen Ellen, an area known as the former home of novelist Jack London. Simon stopped outside a one-story house with a small yard in front and an oak tree that towered over the property.

He got out of the car and entered his house. I watched, my heart rate escalating. While I waited the minutes Simon had requested, I called Dean and filled him in.

"Simon was the one who sold the bottle at the auction and he knows it was counterfeit. He says he's in danger and that I might be, too. I'm just waiting to get a few more counterfeit bottles from him."

"Katie, I don't like this. Why don't you leave and let me handle it?"

"Dean, I promise I'll be careful, but I need to do this. I need to know now."

"Where are you? Give me the address."

"I'm outside Simon's house." I gave him the address as I watched Simon exit the house and head across the lawn to the door of a detached garage.

"I gotta go. I'll call you when I'm done." I put down the phone and opened my car door. A warning bell registered in my stomach and I grabbed my wine opener, pulling out the small knife so it was ready in case I needed it.

I crossed over the driveway and stood at the open side door to the garage. "Simon?"

No reply. I looked around and stepped inside, keeping my hand on the doorframe in case I had to pull myself outside.

The building was the space of a regular two-car garage except there were no cars. Instead there was a long table in the middle covered with crates of wine. At first glance, it looked like a collection at the home of a wine enthusiast. But a garage was not a good place to store wine bottles. It would get too hot and damage them.

Then I noticed several bottles on the table were empty, their labels from notable wineries in Burgundy. They were lined up in an even row next to a jug of pale red wine and two funnels. These weren't old bottles cast away, ready for the recycling bin. These were waiting to be filled.

I stepped to the left, my foot catching on something as I went crashing to the floor, pain ricocheting through my shoulder. If I injured my arm and couldn't carry a tray, I would be out of work for a while. I sat up and rubbed my shoulder. It didn't seem broken and neither did my collarbone. I looked to see what I had tripped over. A crumpled green sweater and a pair of jeans with a solid mass in them. I took a closer look. It was Simon.

"Simon!" I crawled over to him. "Simon, can you hear me?" I placed two fingers on the side of his throat to check for a pulse. There was nothing.

I turned, but a radiating pain on the side of my head knocked me to the floor. Wine was running down my face, my eyes unable to open, the ground spinning beneath my hands and knees.

"Maybe now you'll learn to stay away from my wine," said a deep voice behind me.

I tried to pull myself up, the room a blur as a door closed in the distance, my attacker gone before I could identify him. I sank back to the floor, the world spiraling around me. A dribble of wine crossed my cheek and made its way into my mouth. Although my other senses were shaken, my sense of taste was clear. The wine was one I had tasted before. A peppery Pinot.

TWENTY-SIX

PAIRING SUGGESTION: SYRAH—YAKIMA, WASHINGTON

A red wine with bold flavors and complexity.

❧

I PULLED MYSELF TO my knees, Simon's body coming into focus. My head ached like it would after a night of heavy drinking. Only not my whole head, just specifically the right side. I picked up my wine opener from the floor and held it with the knife out as I surveyed the garage. Boxes lined the side shelves and there was a motorcycle covered with a cloth, but no attacker.

Yet he could be right outside the door, which was now closed, waiting for me to exit. I needed to call the police but my phone was still in the car, a bad habit I needed to break. I scrambled over to Simon and felt his pockets for a cell phone. Nothing.

I glanced up at the door and crawled, standing up against the wall. If the attacker came back, the door would hide me.

But then I saw Simon's phone on the floor not far from his body. I had to make a choice—leave the safety of my position and make the call, or wait. I didn't want to wait.

I ran and picked up the phone. It slipped around in my wine-covered hands as I crawled under the table and dialed 911.

"Help," I whispered to the operator. "I've been attacked and there's—" I looked at Simon. "There's also a fatality."

The sound of a bottle crashing to the floor on the other side of the garage changed my plans to wait online with the operator.

My assailant could still be inside.

It was all the motivation I needed. I had to get outside and in view of other people.

I sprinted to the door and pushed it open, the daylight blinding me as I spun around, ready in case another attack was on the way. The only person in the area was Leanor, exiting her car in the driveway.

"Leanor," I yelled as I ran to her.

"Katie, what are you doing here? You're covered in ... Something?"

"I need help. He might still be here."

"Who? Simon?"

"No, he's ..." I pointed to the garage.

"He's what, Katie? He's what?"

The sound of the squad car made us both turn. It pulled behind Leanor's car, lights flashing, as Deputy Garcia and Deputy Adams hopped out. It was followed by an ambulance.

"Katie, where's Simon?" repeated Leanor with panic in her voice.

Two medics in blue uniforms hopped out of the ambulance.

"Garage. I was in the garage and he was in there—"

Leanor started to run toward the open door.

"But Leanor, the attacker might still be there."

Deputy Garcia ran after her as a medic approached me. "Are you injured?" he asked.

"I'm fine. I was hit on the head, but I'm okay. I'm worried about Simon. He's…" I couldn't say the next word. I didn't want to admit that he was dead.

"I need you to come over here with me," said the medic. He led me to the front steps and started inspecting my head as he conducted a barrage of tests, flashing lights in my eyes and checking my pulse. "How hard were you hit?"

"Hard enough to knock me to my knees."

"I'm going to give you a word to remember, okay? I'm going to ask you this word in a few minutes. If you can remember it, you don't have to go to the hospital. If you can't, you're coming with us. Okay?"

"Okay. What's the word?"

"Apple."

"Seriously? Can't it be something more exciting, like Cabernet? Or Merlot?"

"It's apple. Now, do you have any numbness or tingling?"

"No."

"Do you feel dizzy?"

"No."

"How about sensitivity to light or noise?"

"Honestly, I'm okay. But there's Simon. In the garage. And he's…" I paused.

"Deceased," said Deputy Adams as he approached. "We know. We've checked the area and there's no one else around. You said you were attacked?"

"Yes, someone hit me on the head and killed… killed Simon." My head began to ache more.

Adams glanced at the medic. "How is she?"

"That depends," he replied. "What was the word I gave you?"

"Apple."

"Good job. I don't think she has a concussion. Still, she should be monitored. Head injuries aren't to be taken lightly."

"I know," I said as I took a deep breath. "I'll be careful."

"Is she ready for questions?" asked Adams.

"Sure, if she feels up to it."

I wanted to nod but worried what it would do to my head. "Questions are fine."

"Why were you here?"

"Simon told me to follow him. He had something to tell me."

"About what?"

"It was about the wine. The counterfeit wine." I touched the side of my head. It was throbbing.

"Over the past three days, two people have died and two have been assaulted. It's time for you to leave this to us."

I stayed silent. I knew I wasn't going to stop.

"Did you see who attacked you?"

The throbbing increased. "Don't you think if I saw who it was, I would have already said?"

"I understand you're in pain, Ms. Stillwell, but it's an important question."

"No, I didn't see who attacked me, but it was after I had tripped over Simon's body." My thoughts went to Simon. Poor Simon. But I needed to focus. "It was a man's voice who said that maybe now I would learn to stay away from his wine. That's all I know."

"What do you think he meant by that?"

I shook my head, which wasn't a good idea. "I don't know."

"What else?"

"That was it. Then I called 911."

Deputy Adams nodded and continued to write in his notebook. "What about when you entered the garage? Did you see anything strange or suspicious?"

My headache increased every time Deputy Adams spoke. "Just bottles. But I didn't see anyone waiting for me. If I did, I wouldn't have gone inside. I thought I was about to talk to Simon. He went in the garage just a few moments before I did." I took a deep breath. "This all leads back to the counterfeiting. Simon said that he was in danger and I was, too. And then this happened."

"Who was he in danger from?"

"I don't know, but he said he needed help." I paused. "What if the person who attacked me and Simon and Martin is the same person who poisoned Cooper?" As soon as the word *poison* left my lips, I knew I had made a mistake.

"News spreads pretty fast," remarked Adams.

He had seen me leave Paul's house, so this shouldn't be a surprise. "I guess it does."

Deputy Garcia joined Adams and whispered something to him as he pointed back to the garage.

Adams nodded. "Let's talk about Cooper for a moment."

"I didn't know him that well but he was a nice guy," I said, repeating what I had said at the station the day before.

"That's not what I'm asking," said Adams.

"Did you see anyone touch his wineglass during the evening?" asked Garcia.

"His wineglass?" I raced back to the memory in my mind. "I don't think so."

Deputy Adams glanced at Garcia and back at me.

"What?" I looked at both of them. "We all drank the same wine. That wasn't it."

The deputies seemed to wait to see if I would react. I didn't because I already knew what they were talking about.

"I was the one who poured the wine. But I know what you're getting at. You think it was one of us who poisoned Cooper. Which is why you arrested Paul."

"You're a clever girl," he replied flatly.

"But Paul didn't do it." I didn't mean to say it out loud; it was just a verbal confirmation of what I already knew. I hadn't done anything wrong but the fact that I was on the suspect list unnerved me. Even though they had arrested Paul earlier, we all were under suspicion.

I didn't need any more nights in a cell. I had only ever spent one night in jail and it was enough. Now they had seen me leaving Paul's and at the scene of two attacks. I was showing every indication of being an accomplice or the assailant.

The pain in my head traveled to my stomach as my mind turned with the events of the night Cooper died. I tried to go back to that night and remember if Cooper talked to anyone after dinner, but my memory was fuzzy, most likely from the headache and the stress. He might have told someone else that the wine was fake and that I was the one who figured it out.

And then I let a thought from the back of my mind come to the forefront. The one thought that had been waiting there in the wings, waiting to be acknowledged, but I kept pushing it away. Like when I was with my blind tasting group and didn't want to entertain the idea that the wine was something different than the conclusion I was heading for with my calls. My chest tightened and my breathing became shallow. Paul had been careful not to let anyone know what my profession was that night, but they all knew I was knowledgeable in wine. Cooper wouldn't have been able to tell if the wine was fake, at least not that I knew of, and everyone knew I was sitting next to him at dinner, talking to him in a low whisper.

It was time I acknowledged the possibility, and I swallowed hard as it fully dawned on me: What if the poison had been meant for me?

TWENTY-SEVEN

PAIRING SUGGESTION: BEAUJOLAIS—SAINT-AMOUR, FRANCE

Known as the most romantic Beaujolais,
this red wine is soft, floral, and best served slightly chilled.

❧

"ARE YOU PAYING ATTENTION, Ms. Stillwell?"

I looked at Adams. This moment reminded me of the service portion of the Certified exam. No matter what happens, be ready with an answer. "Well, I do have a head injury." I took a deep breath and rubbed my head. "So what happens now? What about Paul? He's no longer a suspect, right? It wasn't his voice I heard."

"Paul isn't really any of your concern at the moment."

The medic turned his attention to me. "Do you need to go to the hospital?"

"No, I just need some rest. At home."

"If you start to feel nauseated, dizzy, or begin to vomit, you need to go to the hospital. Do you have someone who can stay with you?"

"I'll be fine. I have to get to work now anyway. I'll be super late."

The medic shook his head. "You need to take care of yourself. No work for twenty-four hours and you need someone who can stay with you overnight. Head injuries can be very serious. You fall sleep, you might not wake up again."

Great. Jumping to the worst possible conclusion. "So I can't go to sleep tonight?"

"No, you can go to sleep, but you need to have someone who can monitor you."

The medic continued talking but my attention was distracted as Dean parked on the street.

He ran across the lawn. "Katie, what happened?"

"I'm fine, honest." I stared at him. "Wait, why are you here?"

"I had a bad feeling about you talking to Simon so I wanted to check on you. I started driving down the street and saw the lights." He pointed. "Are you sure you're okay? What's all over your shirt?"

I looked down. The wine from the garage had turned into a dark purple stain.

"It's okay." I pointed to the marks. "It's just wine."

"Detective Dean," said Adams. "We've met before."

"Yes, nice to see you again." Dean shook his hand, then glanced at me and back at Adams. "Can I talk with you for a moment?" They walked to the other side of the lawn while I waited on the steps.

Leanor stumbled out of the house, her black hair disheveled, mascara smeared down her cheeks. She sank down onto the step next to me and grabbed my arm. "Katie, what happened? I came to the house and you were here. Why?" Leanor was a far different person from the one I had met at Paul's house. I wanted to help her but didn't know how.

"I saw Simon at the market. He told me to come here so he could give me some of the bottles and tell me what was going on."

"What bottles?" Leanor stared at me as if she was searching my eyes for answers.

"More counterfeit ones."

"I don't understand." She continued to shake her head. "What did he want to tell you?"

"I don't know. He'd already been hit when I entered the garage."

Leanor stared at her hands as she twisted them around each other. "If he wanted to give you wine, it probably had to do with his work."

"Where does he work?"

"I don't know. Isn't that terrible?" Leanor shook her head. "He always said that he worked for a retailer in Sonoma, but a few years ago I found out that he didn't actually work there. We never talked about the truth. He would always be vague and say, 'just mergers and acquisitions, my dear.' I figured he didn't want me to know, which was fine. We all have secrets." She waved her hand as tears filled her eyes. "I guess it doesn't matter now."

"Was there any hint of what he did?" I asked.

"One time I asked him about it in a roundabout way. He said that it brought in a lot of money and he couldn't stop. He was in too deep and if he told me, it would put me at risk. That was where we left it. Until..."

"Until what?"

Leanor looked at me. "Two weeks ago he said he had a plan and that everything was going to be better. I figured it was just Watkins being Watkins, but then he made a lot of money at the auction."

"You knew he sold wine at the auction?"

"I followed him. I'm a smart girl when I need to be."

"Did you know he sold the bottle of Chateau Clair Bleu? The one that Paul bought?"

She shook her head. "I only knew that he was selling wine. I didn't know the specific ones."

"What about the crates in the garage? Did Simon refill bottles?" I dropped my voice to a whisper. "Do you think he was involved in counterfeit wine?"

"I don't know. But I've never seen those bottles before. They weren't here this morning."

Deputy Adams returned to the porch with Dean by his side. "Ms. Langley, are you ready to talk to us?"

Leanor nodded and stood up.

"Katie, you let us know if you remember anything else. In the meantime, we'll be in touch." He pointed to my head. "I hope you feel better."

I looked from him to Dean, unsure of what was happening.

Adams and Leanor headed into the house as Dean knelt down in front of me, his eyes full of concern and worry. "Are you okay to walk?"

I was unsure whether to act strong or how I was actually feeling, which was a little rattled. I went with a mixture of both. "I can walk. But am I free to go?"

"I've taken responsibility for you." He held out his hand and helped me up.

"Thank you. I really appreciate it."

Dean put his arm around me to help me walk, which felt like half a hug. I didn't want to tell him I was fine to walk on my own. I enjoyed the comfort of his arm and reveled in the scent of his cologne.

"So what happened?" he asked.

"I was attacked. By someone. But I don't know who." I motioned to my car. "I'm parked over there."

"Yes, I see your damaged Jeep." Dean smiled.

Although my head hurt, I appreciated the effort to relieve the tension with humor.

We reached my car and I opened the door and climbed inside.

"Nope, you're not driving," said Dean. "This is just so you can get your phone. You still keep it in the car, right?"

"Yes. But honestly, I'm fine. It's just a smack on the head."

"Nope. You're being taken care of."

I crossed my arms.

"The feeling is foreign to you, isn't it?"

"Yes," I replied, but in a way, it was nice to have him care.

"Besides, I've taken responsibility for you so I'm not letting you out of my sight."

I looked over the steering wheel and then back at him. "Okay then, what's your plan? You can't drive me back to San Francisco. It's too far."

"No, I'm not driving you there. Besides, your apartment may not be safe. Not with the recent break-in and now this."

"Yeah. He said that maybe now I'd learn to stay away from his wine."

"Who said that?"

"I don't know. The guy who hit me. I didn't see his face. And then there was poor Simon ..."

"That's it. I know where I'm taking you."

My head started to ache even more. "Where?"

"You need to be safe. Someone is after you and I have a spare room."

"A spare room?" I looked into his blue eyes. "I can't stay with you, Dean. That's too much of an imposition."

"Why not? You can't go back to your place and I need to watch over you. So you're coming home with me. I like to help out my friends."

"Friends," I repeated under my breath. "But what about my car? I don't want to leave it here."

"No, I'll drive your car and have Deputy Peters bring me back here later. I'm not taking no for an answer. You need to be safe. I can keep you safe. Okay?"

"Okay." I rubbed the side of my head and climbed over into the passenger seat. "This feels like a date."

Dean laughed. "You don't have time to date, remember?"

I nodded and felt a pain in my heart as well as my head.

"You're lucky it's not worse. A head injury can be fatal."

"I know," I replied, but there was no enthusiasm to my voice.

"You can be happy about it, you know."

"Now is not exactly a happy time. I'm a suspect in a murder case, another murder has happened, and now I'm starting to think that someone may be after me. I might have even been the original target."

He glanced at me. "Really?"

"Maybe. I don't know. Cooper sat next to me and … Who knows." I waved dismissively.

"Are you okay?" Dean looked genuinely concerned.

"I'm fine. It just might be time to get a gun."

"You know—"

"I'm kidding," I added, though I wasn't really sure. I had been shooting guns since I was twelve, and my dad would definitely support the idea of me getting one. But I had also heard that you shouldn't own a gun unless you were ready to kill someone. And I wasn't.

"It might not be a bad idea for you to have something to protect yourself. You could start carrying pepper spray."

I shrugged. "I'll think about it, but it wouldn't have helped me today. I didn't even see the guy coming."

"Okay, but keep it in mind. Someone did break into your apartment. And if it was the same person who attacked you today, they know where you live."

I stared at Dean. "Are you trying to scare me?"

"No, just making sure you're aware of the situation."

"I'm aware," I remarked as Dean adjusted the seat and the mirrors. "Very aware."

"At least your original investigation is done," said Dean as he pulled onto the street. "The one for Paul. It looks like Simon was the counterfeiter."

"Why do you say that?"

"Adams showed me his operation in the garage. All of the bottles."

"No, I think someone set him up to take the fall and he interrupted them as it was happening. Leanor said those bottles weren't there this morning."

"You're going to believe Leanor? Someone you said didn't like you when we were at lunch?"

"Yes. She was a close friend of Simon."

"All the more reason for her to lie."

I shook my head. "I don't think so. Simon isn't the counterfeiter. Even though the bottles were at the garage, it's too easy. No, there's something I'm missing. I just don't know what it is."

I stared out the window. The bottle was in Roberto's shop. There would be no reason for Simon to sell it to him only to buy it back and then sell it at the auction. It didn't make sense.

TWENTY-EIGHT

PAIRING SUGGESTION: RIESLING

—COLUMBIA VALLEY, WASHINGTON

A crisp and refreshing wine with notes of apple
and lime in its sweetness.

৵

BEFORE WE REACHED THE winding road that linked Glen Ellen to
Napa, I phoned Bill to tell him I wouldn't be able to make it to work.
Wednesday nights were busy at Trentino, but Bill understood and
said Kurt would cover for me.

When the call was done, I glanced at Dean. "Thanks for taking
care of me today."

"You know I'll be there for you whenever you need me."

"I appreciate it." I stared out the window as we headed into the
mountains, the road climbing as we drove toward Napa.

"Katie, why do you think you might have been the original target
instead of Cooper? Didn't someone push him down the stairs?"

"No, he was poisoned. Everyone was with me in the lounge. No one pushed him. I mean, he could have tripped, but the poison was his cause of death."

"Why do you think it was meant for you?"

"Because I identified the wine as counterfeit. I told Cooper and I think he told someone at the dinner. And that person was the one who created the wine and therefore poisoned him. To silence him." I took a breath. "And now they know I know, too." I leaned forward and stared at the road in front of me. "Simon sold the bottle, Roberto had it before then, but someone at the table was the one who counterfeited it."

"Roberto," said Dean.

"I don't think so. But he did have it. And he's looking into who he bought it from."

"Who else?"

I shrugged. "Henry, Alicia, Leanor, Martin, or Paul."

"Leanor was there today. Could she have attacked you?"

"No, it was a man's voice. At least I'm pretty sure it was. Maybe it was Henry…"

"But why kill someone over wine?"

I looked at Dean. "There's so much at risk. Money, reputations, or maybe even something bigger." There was always something bigger.

My phone beeped with a text. Although the number didn't have a name, I recognized it immediately. You can delete contacts from your phone, but that doesn't mean they'll leave your memory. Kurt.

Hey K, I've emailed you my set of flash cards. Feel better. Peace.

A smile grew on my face. Kurt to the rescue. Of course he hadn't stolen my cards. He wanted to help. He had always wanted to help.

"What are you smiling about?"

I looked up as my smile faded. "What?"

"Who texted you?"

"Oh, Kurt sent me his file of electronic flash cards that I can read on my phone or the computer. At least he says he did. I haven't opened them yet and it's not exactly how I'm used to studying, but it'll be a great help."

"Kurt? I don't think I've heard you mention that name before."

"He's a friend. In my tasting group." I kept my next statement to myself, that he used to be more than a friend. But Dean didn't need to know he was an ex. At least not right now.

Dean slowly nodded. "Just a friend?"

"Yes. Why?"

"You had an odd expression on your face. And you may not like this, but I'm actually starting to be able to read you."

I was tempted to put on my game face, but I let my real feelings show. "We used to date, but it didn't work out. So now we're just friends."

"Why?"

"Why are we friends?"

"No, I mean, why didn't it work out?"

I shifted uncomfortably. "I don't know. Why do relationships end? Life."

"Sorry, I was just curious. Sometimes there's a reason."

I stared at the cars we passed parked along the street. It was time for the truth. It was time to be honest with Dean.

"It was me. I broke it off. I needed to study for my test. Between work and studying, I didn't have time for anything else. It wouldn't have been fair to keep stringing Kurt along. Or fair to me. My sights are set on becoming a Master Sommelier and I'm worried about distractions."

Dean studied me for a moment. "Why do you want this so much?"

"Really? You're asking me that?"

"I want to know what drives you. If you explain the reason for something you desire, it makes more sense to the other person. Then they can understand and perhaps forgive certain things, such as not returning phone calls."

"Makes sense." I nodded. "I want the large red pin. I want to be a Master Sommelier. I want to say that I've made it, that I accomplished something so few people in the entire world have done. The number is less than two hundred and fifty and only a very small percentage are women." I took a deep breath. "And all those people throughout my life, kids in school who teased me, that teacher who said I would never make it, this would prove them wrong. And it would prove my doubts wrong. So I'll keep on going until I have it. No matter how long it takes."

"You'll get there." Dean smiled at me. "I know you will."

"Thanks. Now I have this new set of flash cards so I can keep on studying even though my other cards are gone."

We turned into Yountville, a town located ten minutes north of downtown Napa. Dean stopped the car in front of a duplex.

"Is this where you live?"

"No, I'm taking you to the hospital." I looked at him and he laughed. "Yes, this is where I live." His sense of humor was refreshing after the day I had been through.

Dean opened the front door and we climbed the stairs to a landing, where he unlocked the door to his apartment. The living room had a green couch, a coffee table, a television, and a bookshelf filled with crime novels. The entire place was spotless and twice the size of my small studio.

"The bathroom is on your left. My room is at the far end of the hallway and this here"—Dean pointed to an open door—"is your room for the evening. Or for however long you need it."

I peeked in to see a black futon and a desk. The room was tidy, not an item out of place.

"I'll get you some sheets, a blanket, and a pillow." Dean disappeared for a moment and returned with the items. "I'll call into work so I can stay with you." He unfolded the sheets onto the futon.

"I'm totally fine. Go back to work, I'll be okay here."

Dean pulled the blanket across and placed a pillow at the top. "If I had a mint, I'd put it there." He winked. "How's your head?"

"It's fine. I promise. And I won't fall asleep, in case you're worried."

"Well, I would say watch TV and stay out of trouble, but knowing you, that's not likely." Dean smiled. "But seriously, I would stay away from thinking about everything that's happened. You need to give yourself a break. We'll tackle the next step tomorrow and take a look at Henry. Okay?"

I nodded.

"Since you're so big on studying for your test, why don't you do that? Especially now that you have the flash cards from your friend." There was almost a hint of jealousy in his voice, but I couldn't be sure.

"Good idea." I sat down on the couch. "I'll study my flash cards until you return."

There was a knock on the door. "That will be Deputy Peters to take me to get my car," said Dean. "I'll be back after my shift is over, but hopefully it'll be sooner than that. I'll try and cut out early. Be safe and call me if you don't feel well." He pointed to the side of his head.

"Will do."

Dean left and I sat down with my phone and started flipping through the flash cards. Questions during the exam can cover anything from grape varietals to wineries to geography.

"What are the mountains between France and Spain?" I said out loud. "The Pyrenees," I responded before turning to the answer, the Pyrenees.

I moved to the next question.

"What are the names of Sherry casks?" I knew this one. "Hogheads and Butts," I replied. I continued to the next flash card. "Blind tasting," I said. "What wine do the following characteristics describe? Ruby color, moderate concentration, lush red fruit, strawberry, cherry, raspberry, ripe black cherry, blueberry, pepper ..."

Peppery Pinot. Like the kind I tasted when I was hit on the head at Simon's house. The same wine disguised as a 1975 Chateau Clair Bleu. And the type of Pinot that grows in a specific region in Oregon. At that moment, I knew.

TWENTY-NINE

PAIRING SUGGESTION: PINOTAGE—STELLENBOSCH, SOUTH AFRICA

A dark red wine with bold flavors, ideal for intense situations.

☙

I THOUGHT BACK TO the map of Willamette hanging in Martin's office. Specifically, Ribbon Ridge. Pinot Noir grown in the area had a peppery essence in part due to the marine sedimentary soil and microclimate. Was Martin also responsible for killing Cooper? And Simon, too?

Simon. He said I should take an empty bottle to Alicia, Martin's wife, to get her to talk to me. Maybe he really was trying to help all along. Maybe he was ready to tell me everything and that's why he was killed.

But if so, then Martin knew I was onto him. After all, Martin was the one who told me Simon was the seller. He led me to Simon, but did he also attack me?

I called Dean's cell to tell him. It rang a few times and went to voicemail. I tried again but the result was the same. If he wasn't going to pick up his phone, he at least could have told me. What if I had taken a turn for the worse with my head injury? I sent him a couple of texts and waited. There was no reply.

I could call Deputy Adams, but Martin might already be covering up his whole operation. I was at his office earlier and I didn't see anything unusual, but now I knew what I was looking for. Fake bottles and perhaps wine. Specifically, peppery Pinot.

I called Dean again but there was no answer. Time was running out and if I didn't move fast, Martin might clear out any proof.

I made a decision. I would go to Martin's office to look in the windows and see if there was anything that could be linked to counterfeiting. I would make sure I wasn't noticed, take photos of the evidence, and then drive to the station and report it all to Dean. There was no reason I needed to waste time sitting here when all the evidence could be disappearing.

I wrote Dean a note in case he came back before I got in touch with him and grabbed my car keys. I left the apartment and closed the door behind me, then realized I was still wearing my wine-stained shirt and I didn't have a way to get back in. As I went down the steps, a warning registered deep in my gut. I was stepping out of my safety zone, literally and figuratively. I pushed the feeling aside and got into my car.

———

I arrived at Trager Imports sooner than I anticipated, the two-story building suddenly in front of me. I didn't want my car to draw attention so I did a U-turn and parked a block away at the end of a neighboring vineyard. I shoved my purse under the seat so I could move more quickly and this time I brought my phone as well as my wine opener. My phone was necessary to take pictures and my wine opener was helpful in all situations and my only form of weapon in case I needed one. I tucked the opener into my boot and set off toward the Trager Imports building.

The area was quiet but two lights were on at the rear of the building. A sudden trepidation swept through me. I had no idea what I was doing. I should be back at Dean's apartment, studying and waiting for him to get off work.

I paused as I stared at the building. There was a chance for answers right here, in front of me, before they disappeared. I needed to go through with it. I needed to know.

I crept to the first window. The office was softly lit by the glow of a small lamp on the desk in the center of the room. There was a filing cabinet behind the desk and a potted plant in the corner. A normal office with nothing out of the ordinary and no signs of a counterfeit operation.

I moved to the next window, where all the lights were on. This one was familiar. The desk, the couch, and the map of Oregon on the wall. This was Martin's office.

I grabbed my phone and took a picture of the room, making sure to include the map of Willamette. It wouldn't prove anything, but it would be good to have the photo just in case.

Two small windows around the corner blazed light, illuminating the start of the vineyards behind the building. They were located at the ground level, clearly from a basement.

I crouched and approached a window, careful to keep to the side so I would be out of view if anyone was inside and looked up.

The basement was a small rectangular room with wine barrels lining the far side. Not unusual for a building in Sonoma but as I stared at the barrels, the pieces started to fit. Martin imported bottles of wine, not barrels. If he was indeed forging wine, he would need something to fill the bottles with. A steady amount of wine.

I took a picture of the room with my phone and then moved to the next window to get a better view of the other side.

"Welcome, Katie."

I turned around.

Martin stood a few feet behind me, a smile on his face. "Can I help you with something?"

"No." I stood up, trying to suppress my panic at facing a possible killer. "Just admiring your building."

"It's a beauty, isn't it?"

My phone began to ring. I cringed.

"Go ahead," said Martin. "Answer it."

"No, I'd rather not."

He shook his head and crossed his arms. "Answer it. On speaker."

I looked at the phone, hoping it was Dean and I could signal that I might be in trouble. "Hello?"

"Katherine, it's Roberto."

"Hi Roberto." My hand started to shake.

"I found the name for you. The bottle came from Trager Imports."

"Yeah," I replied as I stared at Martin. "I know."

He grabbed the phone out of my hand and ended the call. "Let's go inside, shall we?" He took a set of keys from his pocket.

"Actually," I said as my heart rate skyrocketed, "I better not. I have to go. Dean will be waiting for me—"

"It's not an option." Martin grabbed my arm and guided me to the door.

THIRTY

PAIRING SUGGESTION: MONASTRELL—JUMILLA, SPAIN

*Also known as Mourvèdre, this grape is often used for blending
but stands on its own in this full-bodied red wine.*

☙

PANIC RUSHED THROUGH ME and I struggled to keep calm as Martin
led me inside. I tried to think of what I could say to get myself out
of this, but I couldn't think of anything convincing enough for him
to let me go.

His grip tightened as he accompanied me down the stairs and
into a doorway, revealing the room I had seen from the window.

He closed the door behind us and released me.

"Welcome to my operation," Martin said as he motioned around
the room. The space I hadn't seen from outside had a long counter
covered with empty wine bottles. Some still had their original labels
while others were blank.

"You didn't need to bring me in here. I didn't need to see this."
My lungs were tight but I kept my hands from shaking.

"Ah, but you did. You were already taking photos from outside." He grinned in a way that I hadn't seen him do before. It was calculating and malicious.

"All I saw were wine barrels. There's nothing strange about a building with barrels. This is wine country, you know." My voice was calm and confident, a stark difference from the fear I was actually feeling.

"I completely agree," replied Martin. "But I'm sure it wouldn't have been long before you had someone else snooping. Which is why I thought it was time to bring you inside." He waved his hand at the bottles. "So what do you think?"

I looked around. "It's a nice operation."

"Is that all you have to say?"

"Bottles and barrels. All looks fine to me." I hoped that would be enough for me to be able to leave, but I knew better.

"You know," said Martin as he leaned against the counter and folded his arms, "I was wondering if you would find us. To be honest, it took you less time than I would have expected. You're a smart girl."

I stayed silent. Every word I said could lead me into more danger.

"My offer from earlier still stands."

"What offer?"

"That we could use someone like you around here. To help us."

I shook my head.

"Oh, Katie. Come on now. Half of life is deceiving people. Look at the news, look at marketing, look at sales. It's all about getting people to believe what you want them to believe. Don't try and tell me you don't do the same thing at Trentino. You tell people about wine in a way that will get them to buy it."

My fear turned to anger. There was everything here to fool innocent people. A complete operation set up to trick wine buyers and now he was asking me to join him. I wanted to tell him about the beauty of real wine and the story behind each bottle. The real story. The history of the wine and the years it was stored, waiting for its moment to shine, and how he was ruining that for innocent buyers. But I knew I had to remain composed in order to get out of there alive.

I walked along the counter, looking at the bottles. "So they pay tons of money for something that's not even real," I said in a calm voice.

Martin laughed. "It's real to them. We're allowing people who love wine to own a bottle they think is something special. Really, we're selling the experience and the joy. They don't know unless they open them, and most of them don't. They store them like trophies in the cellar."

I turned to Martin. "Except for Paul."

His face shifted. "That one was a pity. It was tough that he ended up with the Clair Bleu. I knew he was going to open it so I tried to have my assistant outbid him at the auction, but he continued bidding. If he'd kept it in his cellar, proudly on display, we wouldn't have this problem, now would we?"

The door opened.

"Speaking of," said Martin.

The young man I had seen in the office earlier entered the room along with another gentleman around Martin's age, in his sixties. Panic pulsed through me. I shifted my feet, wondering if I could run to the door and up the stairs before they caught me. Probably not. I still had the wine opener in my boot, but it would do little against the three of them.

"Christopher, I think you've met Katie already."

Christopher nodded and tucked his hand into his vest.

"And this is Vincent, label maker extraordinaire."

I pointed to the blank bottles. "So that's why they're blank. They're waiting for your labels."

Vincent beamed.

"And the three of you do this," I said, unable to withhold my thoughts.

"It's a business," replied Martin. "That's how things are. We all do what we can do in order to put food on the table." He glanced at Christopher. "And sometimes that food is on a yacht in the middle of the ocean."

All three men laughed, but Martin stopped and turned serious. "Katie, this is an opportunity. We'd pay you a lot for your help." He picked up a bottle from the counter. "Besides, you've already helped us."

I stared at the bottle. "I don't understand."

"Don't you recognize it? Take a closer look."

I stepped forward and the label became clear. It was the 1990 Gevrey-Chambertin, Clos Saint-Jacques I had taken to Martin and Alicia's house.

I looked at Martin and finally noticed what I should have seen all along. The bandage that had been on his head earlier was gone and there was no cut, bruise, or mark at all.

"Were you even attacked?"

Martin threw his head back and laughed. "We do what we can to try and throw the scent off the trail. Let's be honest, you were getting a little too close to me. Coming to my house to talk to Alicia. Good thing she called to let me know." Martin placed the bottle back on the counter by the window. "Thanks for that, by the way. It's better to have an original bottle. Then buyers have at least half of what they think they've bought." He smiled. "Besides, not every wine we sell is doctored. Just a few important ones here and there. We provide a nice variety."

Vincent handed something to Martin.

"That's right, I almost forgot. This is for you." He pushed a wad of bills into my hand.

"What's this?"

"Your payout for the bottle. See, there's good money in this."

"That was for Alicia to use the label."

"You think she still does the labels on tiles? You've seen our kitchen. She already has enough tiles. Now she enjoys the finer life, a benefit of our business, and she helps out from time to time." Martin paused. "Let me guess. You've never done anything wrong in your entire life."

"No, that's not it," I replied as the night thirteen years ago went through my mind, when I had broken into a house with the intent to steal.

I looked down at the wad of bills in my hand. It was all twenty-dollar bills and by the size of the bundle, there were a lot. I had to admit, the money felt good in my hand. I could pay off my debts, get my car fixed, easily pay my rent. I had been raised to respect the law and to do things the right way, but that didn't mean it was easy. And here was easy money.

My dad's voice came into my head. *Be on the right side of the law and you can't go wrong.* But I could go wrong. I'd done it once before and I could do it again.

But then my mother's words came through stronger. My mother who had passed away years ago. Her voice drifted through my thoughts. *Always stay true to your dreams.* Wine and becoming a Master Sommelier.

"I don't need this." I held the money out to him, cringing that my fingerprints would be on it.

"Sure you do." He tilted his head sideways. "Maybe you can get a bigger apartment than your tiny place near Golden Gate Park."

The moment clicked. "So it was you. You stole my flash cards."

Martin glanced at Christopher. "I think that was my friend here."

"Why?"

"I'll give your cards back," said Christopher.

"I don't want them back." It surprised me that I didn't want my flash cards back, but in truth, I didn't want anything from the three of them. I wanted to go home. Or at least back to the safety of Dean's apartment.

Martin put his hand up to stop Christopher from replying. "We needed to give you a warning and I figured it was a good way to do it," said Martin. "And I was right. But now that you know everything"—he waved his hand around the room—"it's time for you to work with us." He studied me. "Okay, Katie. What's your decision? Are you in or are you out?"

I looked at the money and then the bottles of wine on the counter. They had already killed Cooper and Simon and I could easily be next. I needed to play along.

"I'm in." I put the money into my pocket. Even the movement of it left me with a bad feeling. "You're right. I need to pay my rent and my bills. This will be good. What do we do next?"

"You're really going to help us?" Martin studied me.

I nodded, my game face hiding the fear inside me. "Of course. As you said, it'll be good money."

There was a familiar noise behind me and I knew exactly what it was. Perhaps my subconscious had heard the click of the safety latch, or maybe it was the noise as it came out of someone's waistband, or it could have been the stillness in the air, but I knew there was a gun and I knew it was aimed at me.

THIRTY-ONE

PAIRING SUGGESTION: ASSYRTIKO—SANTORINI, GREECE

A bone dry white wine made from grapes cultivated in volcanic soil.

ᴕ

I TURNED AROUND TO look at Christopher and Vincent, to see who was holding the gun, but I had been wrong. There wasn't one gun. There were two.

"Seriously? Guns? Come on, guys," I said as my heart pounded. My breathing was shallow and my hands were shaking, so I looped them behind my back. "Listen," I said as I tried to take a breath, "I'm on your side. Let's make wine together."

"I don't trust her," said Vincent.

"Why not?" asked Martin.

"Why should I? We have a good team here, now that Simon's gone."

I felt my game face start to crack. I did my best to keep it on even though my bottom lip trembled. I needed to find a way out of this and my mind began to turn with an idea. "Simon was a traitor, wasn't he?" I knew there was a reason he felt he was in danger and I hoped this was it. "Selling bottles and not giving you guys the cut, am I right?"

Vincent stared, unflinching, the gun still aimed at me. Christopher had his gun in his hand, but it was casually pointed at the floor and I appreciated that.

"He shouldn't have sold that bottle at Red Heart," I continued, "which is why you guys tried to outbid Paul. You didn't want him to open the bottle." I felt a bead of sweat trickle down the side of my face and I hoped they were far enough away that they couldn't see. "It was Simon who messed up. He got greedy. But I think now we have the perfect team with the four of us."

I turned to Martin. I knew him the best out of all of them, though I definitely didn't trust him. "It's going to be great. Right, Martin?" My voice was calm, but I could hear the slightest tremor in it.

"Simon was a fool," said Vincent. "You don't cross us."

"See, now I know that," I replied. The details turned in my mind. "Wait, so did Cooper work for you, too?"

Christopher laughed. "No."

"That was an unplanned casualty," said Martin. "I didn't realize he had such a discerning palate but when he approached me at Paul's that night, I knew he would be a good addition to our team. I asked him to join us." He opened his hands and shrugged. "Cooper said no. He said he was going to tell Paul and that was that. So I took care of it and protected my business."

"So it was you," I remarked. "Since we're being honest here, how exactly did you take care of it?"

"Small, petty Cooper. I invited him to have a drink with me. Except his was laced with a little special something I brought with me. I thought it was best to be prepared since I knew we were opening the Clair Bleu." Martin smiled coldly. "In fact, you were sitting in the same room when I did it. I guess you don't notice everything."

I thought back to the dinner. Alicia talked to me about auctions right before Cooper left to check on the bottle. Alicia, causing a distraction while Martin helped Cooper with a painful and sudden onset of poisoning that explained the fall down the stairs. "But what would it matter if Paul knew about the wine? He knows now."

"Yeah, I didn't bank on you, Katie Stillwell. I thought Cooper was the only one who had figured it out." He shook his head. "Who knew a girl could be the real danger."

I stiffened as my anger boiled.

"Paul would have told everyone about our business," Martin continued. "All of our wine sales would have dried up. Everyone would know what I did. I would lose my reputation." Martin shook his head. "If Cooper hadn't wanted to tell Paul, he'd still be alive." His eyes narrowed. "And if I had known you knew about the wine, I would have taken care of you that night, too."

"But it's a good thing you didn't. Because now I can help you. Let's get started, shall we?" I turned to the bottles on the counter, hoping that the guns were put away. I didn't hear any movement and I could tell at least one was still focused on me. I swallowed hard and tried to appear calm on the exterior as I looked at two bottles, Domaine Hibou and Domaine Garinett, on the table in front of me.

"I don't know," said Vincent.

"What about you, Christopher?" asked Martin.

"If she's as good at wine as you say she is, maybe. If not, we get rid of her."

"Excellent idea," replied Martin. "Let's put her to the test. Go ahead, Christopher."

There was noise around me as the three of them shuffled items, but I didn't move. I remained still, focused on the wall in front of me as my heart rate accelerated.

"We were fine selling our wines, but people are starting to open them," said Christopher. "Now we need to make them taste authentic as well. This is where you come in." He put a glass of red wine on the counter in front of me. "This is our latest batch," he said. "It's supposed to be a 1989 Domaine Hibou."

I stared at the glass. The rim was already too strong for a 1989 vintage. "What do you want me to do?"

"Do you know the Domaine?" asked Christopher.

I wanted to laugh because I had been to the winery on a trip to visit my uncle in France, but I kept my expression neutral. "Yes, I know Hibou very well."

"Tell us if it tastes like their wine."

I picked up the glass, a noticeable shake in my arm. "I can't taste under pressure. Can you please put the guns away?" My comment was met by silence. I took a sip of the wine. It was very fruit forward, like a recent vintage. Nothing like a 1989 Domaine Hibou.

"How is it?" asked Vincent.

I wanted to reply that it was fine and hoped that would be enough to let me go, but I didn't think that would go over well. "It still tastes new," I replied. "You can't hide the fruit that jumps out."

Christopher removed the glass from my hand and gave me another one. "What about this one?"

"Isn't it the same?"

Silence again.

This was much more intense than the blind tasting I would do during my Advanced Sommelier exam. If I could handle this, the exam was going to be a piece of cake. Assuming I lived that long.

"Taste it," said Vincent.

I put the glass to my lips and sipped, not only trying to discern the wine but also trying to figure out a way out of this. "Much better," I said as I put the glass down. "The flavors are muted. It's more believable. I would call this a 1989 Domaine Hibou." Though I hoped my blind tasting skills were still sharp enough to know it was fake.

Christopher picked up the glass and tasted it. "Okay, I agree. She's good," he said.

"Same," replied Vincent. "She can stay."

I breathed a sigh of relief. Perhaps this meant I was going to be on my way soon. But even as I wanted to believe it, I knew that I had seen too much.

"Well done, Katie," said Martin. "Just as I thought, you're going to be very useful to us. Right in time for the auction."

"I'm glad to be part of the team," I lied. "What did you guys add to the wine?"

"The less you know, the better," replied Vincent.

"Agreed. So shall I meet you here again in the morning?"

"Fat chance," said Christopher. "You're not going anywhere."

"You can't keep me here," I said with a laugh in my voice though it was out of fear instead of humor.

"Unfortunately, he's right, Katie," said Martin. "We only need you for forty-eight hours, then we'll clean all of this up."

"You can't do this." I glanced around at the three men. "Someone will come looking for me."

"Who? Paul?" Martin laughed. "I'll call and tell him you've left. That you're working on his project and you'll be back in a few days."

The sound of a bell filled the room.

Martin rolled his eyes. "You've got to be kidding me. Who's at the front door at this hour? It's past eight. People have to know we're closed."

"Did she call the cops?" asked Christopher.

I stayed silent.

"Did you?"

I swallowed. "You have my phone. How could I possibly call the police?"

"Christopher, check it out. Vincent, too. One of you report back."

"You'll be okay with her down here?" said Christopher.

"Christopher, get the door!"

The two men left.

Martin turned to me. "I'm so glad we're working together now. I liked you from the moment I met you. Alicia didn't, but then, there's no accounting for her taste." He grinned as he poured three more glasses. "Want to try the next round of wines?"

I needed to find a way out of this. The wine opener shifted in my boot. The small knife wouldn't do much in attacking Martin. If Christopher and Vincent had guns, Martin probably did as well.

The door swung open.

"It's a cop," said Vincent.

"What does he want?"

"I don't know. When I found out it was a cop, I came right back to get you. Christopher's talking to him."

"Stay here," said Martin, glaring at me.

"You can't leave her down here," said Vincent.

"She's fine. We'll lock the door."

"I'll just continue tasting the wines," I replied.

"Good girl," said Martin. "And just know that if you scream for help, it won't end well for you." He closed the door followed by the sound of the lock turning.

I waited for a moment to make sure they weren't coming back, and then I got to work planning my escape. I pulled at the door handle just in case.

It didn't budge.

I glanced around the room. There were no other doors, but there were two small windows at the top of the room. The same windows I had looked through earlier.

I climbed onto the counter. The windows were near my shoulder level and big enough to crawl through. I pulled at the metal ring below the glass. It wouldn't open.

Upon closer inspection, I could see the seams of the window sealed by the paint. What good was a window if it was painted shut?

I reached into my boot and pulled out my wine opener. It had been a gift years ago from my uncle, my mom's brother who lived in France, and although I had tried more expensive brands, nothing was as reliable as this one. I used it constantly at Trentino when opening wine, but more importantly at the moment, it had a blade.

Using the knife, I worked at the seam of the window, removing the paint that held the two sections together. The knife, which was already due for a sharpening, was dulling quickly—it was meant for cutting the foil off wine bottles, not for removing paint.

When I had made a line around the entire crease, I put the opener on the counter and pulled at the window. Nothing moved. I tried again, using more force. Nothing.

I looked at the second window, but it seemed to be more sealed than the first one. I hopped off the counter and walked around the rest of the room, searching for another escape route, but the concrete block walls left little chance of any additional openings.

I returned to the counter and noticed a flat metal blade behind a group of bottles. Most likely used by Martin and his group to remove wine labels after steaming, it would be ideal to help me.

I climbed back up and pressed the blade into the seam of the window and pushed. It went deeper than my knife and I continued around the entire frame. When I was done, I pulled at the loop. There was tension followed by a cracking sound. The window swung toward me an inch.

I pulled again, creating a large enough gap, and pushed myself through the window until my feet no longer touched the counter below. I kicked my legs as I tried to wiggle through, but the small space of the window seemed to shrink and I wasn't moving forward. I tried to back out but that didn't work either.

I was stuck.

THIRTY-TWO

PAIRING SUGGESTION: SAUVIGNON BLANC

—MARLBOROUGH, NEW ZEALAND

A crisp and acidic wine with notes of gooseberry,
fermented in stainless steel.

✎

THE VINEYARD, AND FREEDOM, were only five feet away, but I wasn't going anywhere. It's possible I had been through worse things in my life than being stuck in the middle of a window facing a vineyard with armed men returning any second, but at that moment, I couldn't think of any.

I started to panic, but I knew that wasn't going to solve anything. Anxiety during my first Certified Sommelier exam caused me to fail. I needed to get it under control so I could figure out how to free myself from this situation before Martin, Christopher, or Vincent returned. I had to calm down.

My breathing was rapid so I tried to look at the vineyards, but the light from the building only illuminated the first few rows. But I knew that when I was out of options, I could create my own. I closed my eyes and pictured rows of vineyards, their organized lines stretching out in front of me, as I breathed in and out. After about a minute, my breathing slowed and I became calmer. Now I needed to get out.

I struggled again but didn't get any farther. I took a deep breath and then felt around the areas of the window keeping me prisoner.

My fingers reached my belt. It was caught on the latch of the window. I remembered what my mom used to say: *Sometimes the thing keeping you from your goal isn't as big as you think.*

I pushed back, unhooked my belt from the latch, and pulled myself through the rest of the window.

I was safely out.

I stood up and pressed myself against the side of the building, away from the window, as I stared out at the night. Complete darkness without the benefit of house lights or street lights. Exactly what I didn't like. In fact, I was frankly afraid of it. It wasn't the fact that I couldn't see; it was the thought of *what* I couldn't see. Objects in my path, danger, attackers. Anything.

But my choices were to stay here and be recaptured or go into the dark. I chose the latter.

I kept low to the ground and started running. I stopped before I got more than ten feet.

My wine opener.

I patted my pants but knew it wasn't there. It was still in the room after I had used it to open the window.

It was my most trusted item and I couldn't leave it behind. It had only been out of my possession once before, when I left it in the wine cellar at Frontier. Tessa had returned it to me a few days later. There would be no returning it this time.

I ran back to the window and pushed it open. My wine opener was on the counter, out of my reach. I pushed in a little farther and when my fingers had just touched the edge of it, the door to the room swung open.

"What?" said Martin as he stood next to Christopher and Vincent. "Get her!"

I grabbed the opener and pulled back out of the window, the latch catching my sleeve and tearing both the fabric and my skin.

I sprinted into the darkness, my legs carrying me to a place I didn't know. I just knew I had to run.

Dark lines came toward me. I was at the vineyard.

"There she is, I see her," said a voice, followed by the beam of a flashlight. I ran harder, entering the row and down the slope, the bare vines to my sides. But I knew right away that it wasn't my smartest move. I was a captive target.

I ran through the dark, my feet pounding on the dirt, the row never ending. I gasped for air, my lungs barely able to expand, my head aching from my earlier injury.

The vineyards, which had always been such a source of calm and order for me, were keeping me in one straight line. A sitting duck.

One of the guys could be right behind, seconds from catching me. I needed to change the situation.

I threw myself on the dirt and rolled under one of the wires, the clipped vines pulling at my hair. I did it a second time, making it under another row of vines. Once I was on the other side, I scrambled to my feet and started running again. I couldn't see anything in front of me, but I didn't have time to check where my followers were.

The row was ending soon. Freedom. I sprinted faster and slammed into something hard at the end of the row. Whatever I hit went crashing down to the ground with me, a grunt coming from it. I had run into a person.

I jumped up to take off again, certain that it was Martin, Christopher, or Vincent, but a scent that I recognized stopped me. An aftershave I knew well.

"Dean? What are you doing here?"

"Looking for you."

I spun around to see if my attacker was behind me. "He was after me. He was chasing me through the vineyard."

"Who was chasing you?"

"One of the counterfeiters. Martin. Christopher. Vincent. I don't know."

Dean pulled out a flashlight and shone down the vineyard. "I don't see anyone. Come on, let's go see who we can find."

"By ourselves?"

"I'll call for backup."

———

Squad cars surrounded the building as I stood next to Dean. It had been a while since my run, but I still couldn't catch my breath.

We waited together while deputies talked to Martin. Dean tentatively put his arm around me at one point to keep me warm, but dropped it almost as soon as it happened.

"Was that you at the door?" I asked.

"Yes, but they said they hadn't seen you."

"Thanks for doing that."

"What?"

"For ringing the bell. It gave me the chance I needed to escape."

A deputy approached us. "According to them, you broke into their cellar through a window."

"I didn't! I *escaped* through that window." My voice quickly disappeared into the night. "What about the bottles? And the barrels? That's what they're using to counterfeit wine."

"Can you walk us through there? So she can verify what she saw?" asked Dean.

The deputy hesitated. "Yes, but you're not allowed to touch anything. Do you understand?"

I nodded.

The three of us headed down to the cellar where the barrels of wine remained, but every single older bottle, both empty and full, had been removed.

"But they were here." I stared at the blank counter. "All the bottles and labels were right here."

"Are you sure you're not just trying to make a scene?" asked Martin as he entered the room. "It's clear that you're not always right."

"You know I'm telling the truth," I seethed.

The deputy stepped between us. "Stop it, both of you."

I touched my head, which had started to ache again from my earlier injury. It was all too much.

"Are you okay? Do you need a doctor?" asked Dean.

"No, I'm fine. Just a headache."

"Yes, I believe you hit your head earlier today, didn't you?" said Martin. "I'd rather not press charges. I think we can put this down to a misunderstanding. Don't you agree, Katie? I'm sure she didn't mean to come in here. I'm happy to drop it."

I stared at Martin, but I knew I didn't have any leverage. I knew I was in danger.

"I think that will be fine," said Dean, replying for me. "Katie, come on." Dean pulled at my arm. "It's time to let Mr. Trager and his employees get on with their evening."

"Don't forget your phone, Katie. You left it on your visit." He handed it to me, a large smirk on his face. "Be safe out there."

When Dean and I reached my car, I turned to him. "You didn't need to speak for me, you know. I can speak for myself."

"I needed to get you out of that situation. It wasn't safe."

I opened my car door and sat down. "I want to go home."

"Not yet."

"What?"

"Two things," said Dean as he held up two fingers. "One, you're going straight back to my place and you're not leaving again. Understand?"

"Okay. What's the second thing?"

"I need my phone."

I raised my shoulders. "I'm not catching on."

"Can you look between the seats? I know it's in here somewhere."

I put my hand between my seat and the center console. There was Dean's phone. "You put your phone in my car?" I handed it to him.

"No. It must have slipped out of my pocket when I drove you to my place earlier today."

"Which is why you didn't answer when I called you."

Dean nodded as he looked at the missed calls on his phone.

"But wait, how did you know it was in here?"

"The same way I knew where you were. I did the phone finder app. It led me to your car. Good thing, too. I thought you might be getting into something dangerous instead of safe at my apartment. I was right." Dean crouched down and looked straight into my eyes. "I believe you. I believe that they're committing fraud and that they held you captive."

"And that they killed Cooper and Simon?"

"Yes." He paused. "But you're a witness and if they're as bad as you say, they're going to come after you. You can stay at my apartment until we figure out what to do."

THIRTY-THREE

PAIRING SUGGESTION: RIESLING—CLARE VALLEY, AUSTRALIA

These dry wines come from an area known for producing excellent Rieslings with crisp acidity and hints of lime without the sweetness.

❧

I AWOKE ON THURSDAY morning to complete silence in the apartment. I walked into the living room, glancing around for Dean but he wasn't there and the door to his room was open.

"Dean?"

No reply. I tried not to think about Martin and his friends. If they found out where Dean lived, they would come here. But they also were more clever than that. They would wait until I was alone and vulnerable. Like I was now.

"Dean?" I repeated. A small amount of panic began in my chest as I walked through the apartment. I reached the kitchen and relief flooded through me as I saw the note on the fridge: *Be right back. Do NOT leave. Kettle should still be warm. Hot chocolate on counter.*

I turned on the kettle. It boiled immediately as I picked up the packet of hot chocolate Dean had left out. The gesture made me smile. It had been a while since we had talked over a cup of hot chocolate, but he had remembered that I preferred it to coffee.

I poured the packet and water into a black mug and took a seat at the table. As much as I enjoyed being around Dean, I wanted to be back in my own apartment. Back in my regular routine. But that wouldn't happen until I was no longer a threat to Martin. He knew where I lived and he knew where I worked. He knew everything about me and I was trapped. Unless I could find a way out.

I thought back to the conversation in the basement at Trager Imports. I was certain one of them, most likely Christopher, had mentioned an upcoming auction.

I took a large sip of the hot chocolate and stared at the copy of the *San Francisco Chronicle* on the table. It was already unfolded so I guessed Dean had been up for a while before me. The liquid burned as it went down my throat, but I was too distracted to care. I grabbed the paper and start flipping through the pages.

I arrived at the list of the week's events and read each one until I saw it. There it was, the Sonoma Wine Auction on Friday from 11am to 4pm at the Monument Hotel.

I picked up my phone and went to the auction's website to preview the items. I didn't have to skim far. Simon may have sold the other bottle under a private party, but Martin had his company proudly listed for lot #14. Trager Imports.

Here was my chance. I could take Martin out in a big way, in front of everyone, and regain my safety. I had twenty-four hours to do it, but I couldn't do it alone. Dean had mentioned the Monument Hotel recently; now I just needed him to come back to the apartment.

I was in the middle of pacing when he opened the door. He held up a brown paper bag. "I brought us breakfast." His expression changed. "You okay?"

"Yes, totally fine. Listen, I know how to fix this whole situation with Martin. I have an idea."

Dean stared at me, his expression still one of concern.

"Will you help me?"

He closed the door and put the bag on the table.

"Dean?"

"I'm listening," he said as he removed packages of tinfoil.

"There's an auction tomorrow in Sonoma and Martin is one of the sellers. I want to go there and—"

"I already know this isn't a good idea," Dean interrupted.

"What am I supposed to do? Just sit here and wait for them to come for me?" I shook my head. "They killed Cooper, they killed Simon, and they're going to kill me," I said as my voice began to tremble.

Dean's face softened. "I'll protect you. I'm going to work with the Sonoma authorities and we'll get this figured out. But until then, I don't want to put you in any more risky situations."

I sat down at the table and Dean sat across from me. He unwrapped a breakfast burrito and passed it to me before unwrapping his own.

"Thanks," I said. "But you can't be around me every second of the day. You have your job and I have mine. I need to take care of this now. I can't live my life in fear." I took a breath. "I'm going to do this no matter what and I'd rather not do it alone." I let a smile come to my face. "And you have to admit, we make a pretty good team."

Dean stared at the table.

I waited, anxious to hear what he was going to say.

"Okay," he replied. Then he met my eyes. "What do you need me to do?"

I grinned. "So you'll help me?"

"Katie, I'd do anything for you. Don't you know that?" His blue eyes sparkled and there was a moment of electricity between us.

"Thank you," I said softly. He had been so kind, taking care of me, letting me stay at his apartment, coming to my rescue. "That means a lot."

He started eating. "So what do you need?" he said between bites.

"Access to the Sonoma Wine Auction tomorrow."

Dean paused. "Why do you think I can get that for you?"

"You mentioned your friend works at the Monument Hotel."

"Yes. Trevor." Dean eyed me suspiciously. "Why do you ask?"

"That's where the wine auction will be."

"Katie."

"Dean, I need you to trust me."

"I do trust you. But if you want to get into the auction, couldn't you just buy a ticket?"

I glanced at my phone. "They're five hundred dollars each."

Dean laughed. "That's pretty pricey."

"No kidding." It was money I didn't have and I didn't want to ask Dean for it. That wasn't a good way to continue our friendship, or whatever it was at the moment. "Any chance Trevor could get me in? Get me a pass or something?"

"I'm not sure, but I'll check."

"Okay, thanks. And one more thing?" I thought about it. "I need the list of specific wines that will be in lot number fourteen. It should be public knowledge, but I can't find it online. The auction would have that."

"I'll call him and see what I can find out."

"Thank you, Dean." I stood up gave him a hug across the table. On the spur of the moment, I kissed him on the cheek.

"Wow," he said. "You should have let me help you sooner."

"Funny." I motioned to the phone. "So you'll call him?"

"Yes, Turbo. Downshift." He grinned and picked up his phone.

By the time we finished breakfast, I had an itemized list of Lot #14 in an email from Trevor. I sat on the couch and scrolled through the list on my phone. The first four bottles didn't strike a chord. But the fifth one did. A 1966 Domaine Garinett. Expensive, rare, and one of the wines that received 100 points from famed wine critic Robert Parker. And also one of the bottles I had seen in Martin's basement. But that wasn't the only place I'd seen it.

I dialed Paul's number. He answered on the first ring.

"Paul, it's Katie."

"Katie," he replied, his voice different than before. Rough with an edge to it.

"I almost have all the details about the Clair Bleu and Cooper's death, but I need a favor first."

"Katie," he repeated, "Martin called me this morning. He said he found you in his basement. You broke in?"

Of course Martin would have called him. He needed any reason he could to stop me. "Paul, I promise I haven't done anything illegal. But I know who killed Cooper."

"Who?" Paul's voice was weak.

I paused as I thought about how to approach it. I didn't want Paul to tell Martin anything until I had a chance to ensure my safety. "I don't want to reveal it until I've proved it one hundred percent. But I need something from you."

There was a long silence. "What could you need?"

"Your 1966 Domaine Garinett."

"Do I have one?"

"It's in your cellar."

Paul muffled a laugh. "I believe you're starting to know my cellar better than I do."

"Can I borrow it? I promise I'll be careful."

Paul sighed. "Katie, I need to take a step back here. I'm out on bail for Cooper's murder and now Martin says that you broke into his building. I can't get more mixed up in this. I'm sorry."

The way he said sorry sounded like he really was, but it left me without the one thing I needed.

"Okay, it's fine. Thanks."

"Katie," he breathed out. "Please be safe."

"I'll try." I put down the phone and looked around the apartment. I needed the same bottle Martin was going to auction off so I could compare them, and the only one I knew of was out of my grasp.

A potential dead end. Just like when allergies act up right before blind tasting. Even though the sense of smell may be compromised, there are still other senses to work with.

And then it came to me. I smiled. I knew who else I could call.

———

Roberto was full of smiles when Dean and I walked into Grand Vino later that afternoon.

"Katherine! I was so happy you called earlier! I'm so fortunate to see you so many times this week. And right before Friday's auction. It's *eccitante*, right? Exciting."

"I agree." Though I wasn't sure why I had said that. I had never been to an auction before. "Roberto, this is Detective Dean."

Roberto shook his hand. "It's wonderful to meet you. Can I pour you a taste of something?"

"No, thanks. We have to get back," Dean replied.

I knew it was a risk leaving his apartment, out in the public eye where Martin, Christopher, or Vincent could see me, but Dean was there to protect me. And I promised we would be quick.

"You're in a rush today?" asked Roberto.

"Something like that," I replied. I decided it was better to leave out the details. "Were you able to get the bottle I called about?"

"I did. Just a moment." Roberto walked behind the counter and pulled out a wooden box slightly larger than a wine bottle. He slid back the cover. "Here it is. A 1966 Domaine Garinett."

I removed the bottle from the box and held it up. The label, which depicted a vineyard, workers in the field, and trees, had been well preserved over the fifty-one years. "Wait, where did it come from?"

"Burgundy."

"No, I mean where did you buy it from."

"Ah, yes, I checked that." He thought for a moment. "A French importer in San Francisco. Very reputable."

"Not Trager Imports?" said Dean.

Roberto laughed. "No."

I stared at the bottle. "And you're certain it's legit?"

He grinned. "One hundred percent."

"Perfect. Thank you." I looked at Roberto. "Are you sure I can take it? I would pay for it if I could . . ."

"Don't be silly, Katherine. I trust you. This is a loan. What will you do with it?"

"I just need to compare it. I'm going to hold it next to the bottle being auctioned to make sure the other one is a fake. And I'll do my best not to open it."

Roberto paused, a look of disbelief on his face. "Katherine, that bottle is worth six thousand dollars."

I heard Dean sigh, but I didn't make eye contact. I focused my attention on the bottle. If I opened it—or worse, broke it—it would take me years to pay for it. But I needed to take the chance.

"I'll be very careful." I placed it back into the box.

Roberto slid the cover on. "Okay." He handed me the box. "You'll bring it back, right?"

"I will. As soon as the auction finishes tomorrow. I promise I'll treat it like my life depends on it." And in a way, it just might.

THIRTY-FOUR

PAIRING SUGGESTION: WHITE PORT—DOURO VALLEY, PORTUGAL

Made from white grapes and very different from regular Port,
this wine is best served chilled.

❧

DEAN AND I PULLED into the parking lot of the Monument Hotel early Friday morning. The black wig we had picked up the day before made my scalp itch and even though I knew it wasn't enough to disguise me from the calculating stares of Martin and his sidekicks, I had to give it a try. The moment they recognized me, I was in trouble. Hopefully the wig would buy me a little time.

"You doing okay?" asked Dean.

"Yeah." I nodded. "I'll be fine. I mean, I'm only risking my career, my freedom, my life." I tried to smile, but I wasn't as good at humor as Dean.

"I'm concerned for you," he said. "But I also believe in you. You can do this."

"Thanks."

I picked up the satchel bag containing the wine. The protective box made the bag awkward and I didn't like it. "This isn't going to work." I pulled out the box and removed the 1966 Domaine Garinett.

"Don't you need to keep it safe?"

"Yes," I replied as I wrapped the bottle in my sweater and put it back into the bag. "But I need it to look like I'm not carrying anything." I slung the bag across my chest.

"Ready?"

"Ready." I opened the car door.

"Please be careful," said Dean. "I'll be watching you from a distance."

"Thanks." I got out and headed toward the side of the hotel, where the service doors to the ballrooms were located.

As promised, a tall man stood guarding the side entrance.

"Hi," I said. "Trevor, right? I'm Katie, Dean's friend. Thanks again for the list."

The man glanced around. "Sorry, Trevor called in sick."

"Seriously?"

"One hundred and two fever. Is there something I can help you with?"

I paused. "Trevor was going to let me into the auction."

"Guest passes are up at the front. Check there."

"No," I said. "I mean, through here."

The man stared at me. "No one is allowed through here except employees. You want a guest pass? Go to the front like everyone else."

I was literally ten feet away from proving everything and regaining my safety, but now I was stuck.

"Any chance you're going to be taking a break in the next few minutes?" I asked, holding back my next thought about leaving the door unattended. I figured it was worth a try.

He shook his head.

If I were stuck in the Advanced Exam, unable to remove the cork from the bottle for the decanting, I wouldn't give up. I would get additional tools. Because it's not that everything in the test needs to go right. You can still pass when things go wrong, but you need to demonstrate that you can handle every situation and get it figured out.

I stood near the side of the building and watched as guests walked into the entrance of the auction. It didn't start for forty minutes, but it seemed that most people decided to arrive early, and the attendants checked every single ticket. There was no way I could sneak in. But like everything in life, I needed to wait for an opportunity. And I needed to be wise about it.

A few minutes later, I had it. A woman in her fifties struggled to carry two flower arrangements from her car.

"Can I help you?" I said as I approached.

The woman looked at me wide-eyed before relief flooded her face. "Yes, thank you. I'm running late. This day has been a mess."

I took one of the arrangements from her and shifted my weight to carry the heavy vase filled with red and white roses, gladiolus, lilies, and chrysanthemums. "Where are we going?" I asked, even though I knew we were going into the auction. I didn't want to seem too knowledgeable.

"Right in here." She walked in front of me.

A knot formed in my stomach as we approached the ticket takers.

"Carrie, so sorry I'm late. Which room do these go in?"

"Main room," said Carrie, the attendant, as she glanced suspiciously at me.

"Thanks," said my new friend and she walked past Carrie. I followed only a step behind, not making eye contact with her.

We put the arrangements on the table behind the podium.

"Thank you so much for your help," she said.

"You're welcome. Do you need a hand with anything else?"

She glanced around. "No, I think I'm fine." She looked at me. "You have a ticket, right?"

I patted my bag. "Right here. In fact, I'll go get my paddle now."

"Great." She smiled. "Thanks again for your help."

I drifted away, walking slowly so as to not arouse suspicion. When she turned away, I stepped into the back room of the auction.

Bottles and cases of wine were lined up, each one with a tag indicating the lot number. There were two other people in the room, a man and a woman, who stood chatting in the corner. I smiled and nodded and pretended I had an official reason to be there. I've often found in life that if you pretend you belong there, people think you do.

I walked along the tables until I found the bottles being auctioned by Trager Imports. In the middle of the group, there it was. The 1966 Domaine Garinett.

While the two people continued talking, I removed the borrowed bottle from my bag and compared them. The vineyard, the trees, and the workers in the field all looked identical to the other label. Could it be that Martin's bottle *was* actually a 1966 Domaine Garinett?

No. I had to trust myself.

I placed the bottles next to each other, making sure to keep Roberto's bottle to the right, and stared at them, studying every little detail. And then I found it.

The label was placed higher on Martin's bottle and the ullage, the level of wine, was high in the neck—not representative of a 1966 bottle that would have lost wine over the years. It was enough to give me the confidence to proceed with my next step. The step that could either fix everything or ruin it.

I put Roberto's wine back in my bag and moved into the main auction room. It was nearly full but I found a seat in the fifth row, on the side. If Martin or Christopher saw me, they would have me removed, or something worse, I was certain of it. I kept my head low and didn't relax until the auction began.

Thirteen lots were before the bottles from Trager Imports and several times I was tempted to raise my own hand. Not that I had the money to pay for the wine, but I wanted to own the bottles. However, I didn't have an auction paddle and there was no way I could afford to bid.

The lot from Trager Imports began and I wondered how many of the first few bottles were also counterfeit.

"You're not bidding," said the gentleman next to me.

"I might," I replied, not wanting to reveal my motives.

"Where's your paddle? You can borrow mine if you want." He shifted his number 55 toward me. "But you'd have to pay me back." He grinned.

"Thank you." I didn't reach for the paddle. I didn't want anyone to mistake my movements for bidding. I didn't want attention on me. Not yet.

"Next up on our auction," said the auctioneer. "We have a 1966 Domaine Garinett, which received one hundred points from Robert Parker."

This was it.

I stood up, pushing down my anxiety as I did. "Excuse me, I have a problem with this next bottle."

The auctioneer looked surprised. "Who is that?"

I walked down the side aisle, ignoring the tightness in my chest. "I know for a fact that this bottle is counterfeit."

The auctioneer glanced to an official on his right.

"Sorry, everyone," I said as I stepped onto the stage. "I know you don't know who I am, but you'll want to hear this before you bid."

The auctioneer put his hand up for security, but I shook my head.

"It's okay." I leaned toward him and whispered, "This bottle is fake. It's been doctored to look like a 1966 Domaine Garinett but it's not." I picked up the bottle from the stand and turned to the crowd. "The wine inside this is an Oregon Pinot and a recent vintage at that. The seller is trying to fool you."

"Put it down," said the auctioneer. "That's a valuable bottle of 1966 Domaine Garinett."

"Actually, it's not. And I'm about to prove it." I pulled out my wine opener.

"If you open that bottle," said the auctioneer. "You're paying for it."

That's when I felt arms around me. I was being tackled by security, or possibly Martin, but I hoped it was the former.

The satchel bag hit the ground before I fell on top of it. I winced from the pain but also because I hoped the bottle, the expensive wine I had borrowed from Roberto, was still intact.

"Give me a moment," I said, my voice muffled from the stage as my cheek pressed against the floor with the force of my captor. "I can prove it. Just open the bottle and taste it. You'll see."

My arms were pinned behind my back and I was pulled onto my knees, the black wig on the ground in front of me.

"Just taste it!" I yelled. "Please, just taste it."

"Wait," said a voice from the audience. "I'll buy the bottle. Then she can open it."

THIRTY-FIVE

PAIRING SUGGESTION: ICEWINE—ONTARIO, CANADA

A sweet, honeyed wine created by leaving the grapes on the vines until they freeze in the winter and then pressing them while frozen.

☙

I LOOKED TOWARD THE origin of the voice. There was Dean, standing in the middle of the rows, holding up his wallet.

"Let me buy it."

"But sir," said the auctioneer. "This is an auction. You have to bid."

Dean looked around. "Great, let's continue and start the bidding. I want to make the first bid and the last." He glanced at me. "And then I want Katie to open the bottle."

The auctioneer didn't move. "But you don't have a paddle."

"Can someone get me a paddle?"

The auctioneer whispered to an official as I was pulled to the side of the room, the security officer's hand still on my arm.

Four attendants moved around and one of them briefly spoke with Dean before he approached me.

"You okay?"

I nodded.

"Here's your paddle and here's your credit card back," said an attendant as she handed both to Dean. The security officer dropped his grip on my arm.

I rubbed the space where he had held me. "Dean, you don't have to do this."

"Yes, I do."

"But it's going to go too high. You can't afford this."

He looked at me, his blue eyes staring deeply into mine. "I trust you."

"Sorry for the interruption," said the auctioneer from the stage. "Now, let's start the bidding for the 1966 Domaine Garinett at four hundred dollars."

"Four hundred," said Dean as he held up his paddle.

"We have four. Do we have five?"

My heart pounded as Dean continued to bid, battling against one other bidder. I didn't think anyone would want to bid on it, knowing there was a chance it was counterfeit. I glanced around Dean to see who it was, but I didn't recognize the bidder.

Dean raised his paddle and bid again. It continued this way until there was silence.

"Going," said the auctioneer. "Going, gone. Sold!" The auctioneer banged his gavel. "For four thousand five hundred to, um, what's your name?"

"Dean."

"To Dean."

"Thank you," he replied. "And now I would like Katie to open it."

"This isn't part of the agenda," said the auctioneer.

*

"It will only take a moment," I replied as I climbed onto the stage and picked up the bottle. I turned to the room of two hundred people. Martin walked in and stood against the back wall. He scowled at me.

As I held up the wine, Martin removed his cell phone from his pocket and started scrolling through it. I had minutes, if that, to prove my point before one of his crooked employees arrived, if they weren't already here.

"You know the seller is Martin Trager but what you don't know is that Trager Imports has been counterfeiting wines. The 1975 Chateau Clair Bleu purchased by Paul Rafferty two weeks ago was a fake." I held up the bottle. "And this one is, too."

I took out my wine opener and tried to cut off the foil, but it was dull from the window. I continued and though the line was ragged, I was able to make a cut all the way around the neck of the bottle.

The crowd began to whisper but I pressed on, revealing the top of the cork. It looked strong, a confirmation of my suspicions that I was correct.

"This cork should be fifty-one years old, yet it appears to be in great condition. As if it were new. You'll see. I don't even need an ah-so for this." I inserted my opener into the cork as flashbulbs from the media went off.

This was the moment I could lose everything: my job, my reputation, and a massive amount of money to pay Dean back for the bottle. Money that I didn't have. But I knew I was right. I safely removed the cork and my fears subsided. The entire cork was in excellent condition.

"See, the thing is, they think no one will ever open these bottles. Most of the time they're bought to be kept as trophies, special mementos to remain in the cellars and never opened." I motioned to

Dean, who stepped onto the stage and handed me a glass before returning to the side.

I poured a good amount and held up the glass, the red wine shining in the indoor light. The rim wasn't faded; it was strong like a new wine and it lacked the slight orange color found in an older Pinot Noir. I put the glass to my lips and in front of an audience of two hundred people waiting to see if I had ruined my career, I sipped the wine.

There it was, the familiar taste of peppery Pinot. I was right.

I held up the bottle and the glass. "This wine has all the clear indicators of a recent vintage. Not one from 1966. I know that if you proceed to test this wine, you will find that it comes from an Oregon winery owned by Martin Trager. And furthermore, you'll find that it's been tampered with, adding who knows what to make it resemble a 1966 Domaine Garinett."

Someone from the audience began to clap. I looked up and there was Martin, standing in the middle of the aisle, his hands together. "Nice try, Katie. Sorry about this folks, but you've just heard a lie from someone who attacked me, broke into my cellar, and killed my employee Simon. Don't put any worth into what she's saying. Now, if we can get security to remove her, we can continue with the auction."

"No," I replied. "I'm right. If someone will come up here and taste this wine, they will know I'm telling the truth. Someone who's experienced with older wines."

No one moved.

"Please. I need one person to confirm this." I looked out at the crowd and then at the auctioneer.

"Please," I repeated. It sounded like I was pleading, and perhaps I was.

The auctioneer hesitated and then took my glass. He stared at the wine, glanced out at the crowd, and then swirled, sniffed, and sipped it.

My heart pounded in my chest as I waited for him to announce his conclusion. If he didn't agree with me, I was sunk.

He leaned into the microphone. "I can't believe I'm going to say this, but she's right. This wine is counterfeit."

A gasp rippled throughout the audience.

Martin turned and walked to the back door, but Dean was there, handcuffs in hand.

I looked at the bottle, my hand trembling as I held it. Wines like these were not made to be opened. And this one never would have been if it weren't for me.

THIRTY-SIX

❧

AFTER DEAN DROVE MARTIN away in the squad car, I returned to the ballroom. The excitement had died down and after a fifteen-minute recess, the auction resumed. I waited in the back as bottles reached price tags into the thousands.

Someone stood up and shuffled along the row. It was Paul. He reached the aisle and walked toward me.

"Katie," he said as he approached.

"Paul, I didn't know you were here."

"It's a wine auction. Of course I'm here," he said, followed by his familiar cough.

The auctioneer looked at us.

"Let's go in the other room," I whispered, and we exited into the hallway. "Since you're here, I'm assuming you saw everything. With Martin, I mean."

Paul nodded. "Yes," he said as he closed his eyes. "I saw it all."

"I'm really sorry that it was Martin all along," I said. "I know that has to be tough."

He paused. "Sometimes," he finally said, "you don't know who you can trust. Even a best friend." He looked crestfallen and tired. "I'm so sorry I put you in danger."

"It's okay. I'm glad I was able to help you." I motioned to the bottle he held in his left hand. "What did you buy? Was that from today?"

"Oh yes, this." Paul lifted the bottle and showed it to me. It was a 1975 Chateau Clair Bleu. "It happened earlier."

I had been so focused on the 1966 Domaine Garinett, I hadn't even noticed that a 1975 Chateau Clair Bleu was on the auction list.

"Paul, I'm so happy for you."

"There was no bidding war this time either. I bought it for only eight thousand dollars." Paul beamed. "It's real this time. The seller is very reputable and the bottle has been traced directly back to Chateau Clair Bleu. There are papers to prove it."

"I'm glad, Paul. You deserve it."

He glanced at the bottle and then looked at me. "I'm still going to open it, just like before."

I nodded. "After all, it's been waiting forty-two years to be opened and tell its story. I know you'll enjoy it. Perhaps even more so this time. Because you know it's real."

"Katie, I've been thinking. I could really use some help in expanding my wine collection. Someone who could help me track down certain bottles, and of course make sure they're the real deal. It would only be a few hours a month, but I'll make it worth your time. Are you interested?"

I thought about my job at Trentino and my study plans for the Advanced Exam. Then I thought about paying my bills and getting my car fixed. "I'd love to. Thank you." I smiled as relief flooded through me.

"Wonderful. We'll be in touch." He coughed.

"Are you sure you're okay?"

"I'm fine. Weak lungs, that's all. I'll be around for a long time." He smiled and held up the wine. "Next week I'd like you to be the one to open the Clair Bleu. How does that sound?"

I looked at the bottle, knowing that it came from a reputable seller and would not only be a real bottle of Chateau Clair Bleu, but would also mean a great deal to Paul. "It would be an honor."

"But no dinner at the house this time." He smiled. "I'm going to bring it into Trentino along with a check for the work you've already done." He perked up and looked toward the ballroom. "I think the next bottle I want to buy is up."

"Go, go bid. We'll talk soon."

"Thanks again, Katie. For everything." Paul returned to the room.

I hesitated in the lobby for a moment but decided not to return to the auction. It had been a big day already and I needed some fresh air.

I walked outside and saw Dean at the bottom of the steps.

"Hey," I said as I approached him. "What are you still doing here? Where's Martin?"

"He's at the station with Garcia. I came back after taking him. They'll want to get your statement after you're done here."

"What about Vincent and Christopher? Are you here for them?"

"No, Adams is picking them up at Trager Imports right now. He also said he wants to question Alicia."

"Good." I paused. "Am I still in danger?"

"No, I don't think so. I think it's all going to be okay. I just wanted to see you before you headed to San Francisco. I didn't want to give you the chance to dodge my calls now that this case is over."

"That wouldn't have happened. Not this time."

"I know, I know." Dean smiled. "But I had to make sure."

A breeze blew past us and rustled the trees around the parking lot.

"I was really proud of you in there," said Dean. "The Palate."

"Thanks." I glanced back at the Monument Hotel. "I couldn't have done it without you. Thank you. And I'm sorry about the cost."

"I'm sure I won't have to pay. The bottle was counterfeit. Do you still have Roberto's bottle?"

"It's here." I tapped my bag. "I'm going to take it to his shop right now. I can't wait until it's no longer in my possession. I can't afford to replace it. In fact, I can't afford anything."

"I was thinking, maybe we could find you a job out in Napa?"

I smiled. "Actually, Paul Rafferty said he would love for me to work for him part-time. That way I could keep my job at Trentino but still get extra money."

"Paul lives in Sonoma Valley, right? That's pretty close to Napa." Dean shifted his stance.

"Yes," I replied. "Not too far." I smiled.

Dean looked at me with a sheepish grin. "That's good news. So the real reason I'm back here is because I wanted to ask you something."

"Okay." I waited as my stomach flipped.

"Food," he replied.

"That's your question?"

"Sorta." He smiled. "Would you like to go to dinner with me?"

A smile spread across my face. "Yes, but I can't tonight. I have work. I've missed my last two shifts and I don't want Bill to give my job away."

"Okay." Dean adjusted his expression but his smile remained. "How about tomorrow? Or another night? I'm happy to take a rain check."

I stared at him as the wheels turned in my mind. "This isn't just dinner, is it?"

He shifted. "No, this would be a date. An actual first date."

I stared at Dean, his blond hair swept softly over his eyes. "Are you sure? My job takes nights and weekends away. Combine that with studying and I don't end up with a lot of free time. That frustrates people."

He nodded as he looked at the ground. "You do have your job. And you are studying for your Advanced Exam. And some people might get frustrated." He looked up and smiled. "But some may not. Some may appreciate the time they do get to spend with you. So…"

"So…" I said with a smile.

"Would you like to go out with me?"

I knew the answer already, though it took me a second to say it. "Absolutely."

THE END